The Paradise Bird Tattoo

The Paradise Bird Tattoo

CHOUKITSU KURUMATANI

Translated by Kenneth J. Bryson

COUNTERPOINT · BERKELEY

Original title: Akame Shijuyataki shinju misui
Copyright © Choukitsu Kurumatani, 1998
Originally published in Japan by Bungei Shunju, Tokyo.
English translation © Kenneth J. Bryson, 2009

All rights reserved.This book has been selected by the Japanese Literature Publishing Project (JLPP), an initiative of the Agency for Cultural Affairs of Japan.

This is a work of fiction. Names, characters, places, and incidents are the product of the author's imagination or are used fictitiously. Any resemblance to actual persons, living or dead, is entirely coincidental.

Library of Congress Cataloging-in-Publication Data is available.

Hardcover ISBN 978-1-58243-703-3
Paperback ISBN 978-1-58243-704-0

Printed in the United States of America

COUNTERPOINT
1919 Fifth Street
Berkeley, CA 94710

www.counterpointpress.com

Distributed by Publishers Group West
Designed and typeset by Gopa & Ted2, Inc.

10 9 8 7 6 5 4 3 2 1

The Paradise Bird Tattoo

1

At the Kagurazaka subway station in Tokyo, several years ago, I read these words chalked on the message board:

> Club activities are cancelled because our buddy Hirakawa sang one of Yoshida Takurō's ballads "In Praise of Love" with his friend Asada. Hirakawa is dead.

Another night, more than a dozen years ago, I saw this written on the message board at Nishi-Motomachi Station on the Hanshin line in Kobe:

> I waited for you till 9:30. You're cruel. Akiko.

Neither incident had anything to do with me, but the memory of those spooky chalked words has haunted me ever since. Maybe it was because of a sense that I had come into direct contact with a sorrow that almost bordered on hate.

I went broke in Tokyo when I was near the end of my twenties. I had nothing left to my name; I spent the next nine years down-and-out, living hand to mouth from one day to the next.

It was late one night during one of those nine years when I sat on that bench in Nishi-Motomachi Station, burned out, with nowhere to go and no place to call home. It was a cold night, just after New Year's, and an icy wind was blowing. Actually, at the time, the self-abandonment that had left me with no place of my own but that station bench might have been a sort of salvation for me. There are women who can make a living on their own after quitting a company job, and then again there are men who can't. I was one of those weak-willed men.

But in the summer of 1983 I went back to Tokyo, penniless as I was, and started another office job that I got through someone's kindness. I was thankful, after having been trapped in the lowest depths of poverty, but I felt a secret twinge of disappointment at being in an office job again after having once turned my back on that life.

It was really hot that summer. I had rented a bare, unfurnished apartment on a back street in the Koishikawa-Sasugayachō district, but all I had to put in it was a cloth bundle tossed into a corner with my underwear and some other things. I was supposed to start work the next morning but didn't have the money to buy the suit and shoes I needed. I had been living for nine years in wooden geta clogs, an outcast from society. It was eleven years since I last held down a job. I was thirty-eight years old already; although I took an occasional interest in women during that time, I had never enjoyed either the pleasures or the terrors of having a wife and children. Being alone like that was what made it possible for me to live as an outcast yet manage not to die by the wayside and instead come back to Tokyo. An office job, or whatever, it made no difference. I needed the money, and appearances didn't matter as long as I had a job.

It was sweltering indoors, but I knew all too well that I had gone cold—a lost cause. I no longer expected anything from myself, yet I couldn't say that aloud to save my life. Here I was, a man who had lost his place in society and been the object of everyone's scorn, yet accepted that condition and crawled along in it like a crab; now I had come back to a life of dressing in suits and shoes. Without doubt, this was the behavior of someone who knows no shame—a feckless pushover. As I sat with both hands flat in front of me on the apartment's wooden floor, a small spider crawled up on the back of one hand and slowly walked across it.

Back then, there was still some energy left in my system. True, the grim solitude sometimes made itself felt somewhere in the depths of my being, but I could still bear it. In the spring of my forty-third year, however, I went to work in spite of hematuria and a bad case of chills and collapsed at the office from overwork; I spent over fifty days in the hospital with hepatitis. Superstition holds that forty-three is an unlucky age for a man, misfortune lingering after what we call the "great crisis year" of forty-two. Now, two years later, I've developed ischemic heart failure and can no longer live from day to day without the medications my doctor prescribes.

I will probably never recover and will end up one day the way the newspapers talk about some people when they are found— *Old man dies alone; skeletal remains discovered.* But that's fine— or so I rashly resolved, at least in my head. That I possess no true mental resolve, however, should be obvious just from the fact that I came back to Tokyo, lured by a tempting story. If push really came to shove, I would probably have a major struggle. I'll never forget the turmoil I felt in my mind two years ago when I heard the doctor on the other side of the white curtain whispering, "I need to speak to you. Please call his wife immediately."

The person who had brought me to the hospital told him, "Oh, he doesn't have a wife."

Thus nothing out of the ordinary happened to me for the past seven years since I returned to Tokyo, although my physical health was steadily deteriorating; the daily routine of trips to and from the office was a state of peace, if you want to call it that: no particular joys or sorrows, nothing that caused my soul to tremble. The days went by quickly and predictably. At the office, I had to deal with the inevitable human relationships that come with the territory; otherwise I had nothing to do with others. I usually spent my days off totally wiped out, sleeping like a corpse in my apartment. Nevertheless, the corpse would put on its suit and shoes and go back to work again, just to live a little longer.

I cut a weird figure in people's eyes with my habitually close-cropped hair and my papers kept in a cloth shoulder bag. They talked about me behind my back; they laughed at me; they were disgusted with me. At times I even made them angry, for no apparent reason.

None of that made any difference to me. I had no telephone connection, no television set, no furniture; the rooms in my apartment remained as bare as they were when I first came back to Tokyo. In the midst of such a slovenly daily routine, the pain of throwing away a dead wildflower that I had kept in an empty bottle, watching it as it faded day by day, was a spiritual ray of light. Whatever the situation in the core of my being, the one thing I could not discard was the desire to abandon all connections with the world. Throwing myself into work with all my spirit was, for what it was worth, a way to abandon the world. In the most frigid part of my psyche lurked an unblinking figure of despair that said *what the hell.*

Some people would call my situation a state of spiritual decay. There's no fundamental meaning or value in human existence, however. In that respect, there's no difference between us and birds or beasts, insects or fish. It's just that people have made up stories to make it sound as though human life has meaning or value. Hence, there's no valid basis for writing these very words. Still, in order to live, we inevitably have to question the meaning of life. For me, life meant living this contradiction in words.

At night on New Year's Day one year, I wrote this in my notebook:

> The New Year is here, but I have nowhere to go or return to. No one comes to visit, and I have no interest in visiting anyone. After noon, I go for a walk along the river bank in Senju. The long expanse of dead rushes is bleak; the cold river flows on, black, shining, and unctuous. From a spot amid the rushes rises a thin plume of smoke. Approaching, I find a man huddled in a heap of refuse; he has piled up some stones and is cooking stew in an iron pot. His eyes are clear.

It was along the Arakawa Canal, near where the Keisei railway bridge crosses overhead. The following New Year's Day, I again walked along the wind-swept riverbank and waded into the dry rushes. This time, he glared at me with a fierce anger in his eyes. He stands out in my memory of those days of monotonous routine, an unforgettable figure.

Speaking of unforgettable strangers: one day last year during the fall rains, I was walking with my umbrella on the road outside the wall of the Koishikawa Botanical Garden when an unfamiliar woman called out to me: "Where are you headed?"

Without thinking, I answered, "To the library."

"Then I'll come with you."

She came straight up to me, acting as if we already knew each other well, and began to walk alongside. The lack of caution in her behavior made me uneasy. Fortyish and wearing no makeup, she did not strike me as the ordinary housewife type. When I speeded up, so did she; when I returned to a normal pace, she did the same without saying a word. She seemed determined to stick with me, no matter what.

When we got to the library, I felt relieved as she drifted off to a different section of the stacks. She showed up again a little while later, though. Opening up a thick volume of natural history in front of me, she asked, "Would you believe these worms are edible?"

I looked and saw the illustration of a large green caterpillar, in full color.

When I stared at her face in surprise, she said, "Oh, no, we lived on them." Her eyes were bloodshot. Her tense tone of voice sent a chill through me, setting my hair on end. Without doubt I, too, had "lived on worms."

Twelve years before, I had been eking out a living sticking bits of animal organs and chicken meat onto skewers, day after day, in a neighborhood with rusty tin rain gutters near Deyashiki Station on the Hanshin Railway line. At the time, it was six years since I had embarked on life as a piece of drifting debris, counting two years out of work in Tokyo.

It began with me quitting my job without any prospects of future employment. I did stints as a shoe-check clerk at an inn in Himeji and then as kitchen help in a Kyoto restaurant, in an *okonomiyaki* place in Kobe that was a hangout of *yakuza* gangsters, and in a cheap drinking joint in Nishinomiya catering to horse racing fans. After a run of such sketchy work, so different from my days at the advertising agency in Tokyo's central business district, I ended up in the Deyashiki district of Amagasaki.

The people of Amagasaki refer to their city, with a peculiar kind of fondness, as "Ama." Originally a feudal castle town, by the 1920s it had grown into an industrial zone with huge steel mills lining the seashore. Immigrants come to find jobs from remote prefectures like Kagoshima and Okinawa and even from Korea, making up a good 20 percent of the city's population and leaving a strong mark on its urban character. The oldest part of the city surrounds the Hanshin Railway's Amagasaki Station; walking westward from there along busy commercial streets, you gradually enter a district with no human vitality. This is Deyashiki. To some extent, every modern city is a gathering ground for drifters who gravitate in to look for work. You might say that Amagasaki wears this quality on its sleeve. I was also one of those who had come here after running out of luck.

While working not far away in that cheap bar in Nishinomiya, I heard people say, ". . . you know, there's a lot of 'hataraki-do' around here." That was what they called the day laborers and hired hands around Amagasaki—"working stiffs." They were probably men like me, without families, who wandered around in front of Deyashiki Station on days when they were unable to find work. They sat in circles by the roadside in the middle of the day, drinking themselves blind. They sang, fought, and got filthy; some sprawled, asleep, with their rubber boots on. The morning after a rained-out night game at Nishinomiya baseball stadium, vendors would pull up in trucks loaded with boxed meals that would have been sold at the ballpark the night before. For a mere twenty or thirty yen each, they sold these meals off the back of their trucks to the down-and-outers and the women who hung about them like flies. With the lids off, it was obvious these meals were already starting to go bad in the summer heat; knowing this full well, those men and women crowded around for them nevertheless. I was in those crowds, too. Stark scenes like this come to mind when people say "Ama," along with the immediate sense of sadness that accompanies an absence of vitality.

2

I was standing on the platform at Amagasaki Station on the Hanshin Railway line, my belongings tied up in a single cloth bundle swinging in my hand. The air around you never feels so fresh and clean as when you've arrived in a strange town for the first time, but you also get the unsettling feeling that you're about to be swallowed up by the unfamiliarity of the place. When I walked down to the Kamo River in Kyoto early that same morning after leaving my acquaintance's house in the Koyama-Hananoki-chō district there, I had found it completely frozen over. In Amagasaki, it was raining with a mix of sleet. From the sky, a bitterly cold air mass moving south from Siberia was crushing down onto the Japanese island chain. Although I had been off the train for a while, I stood there unable to move; this was my first time here, but from the people moving around me I could already sense in every cell of my body the abnormal atmosphere that makes this town what it is. A man approached me without warning.

"Got a light, bud?" he said.

With one look, I could tell that he didn't seem the type who makes a normal living. His pale face had a bluish cast where he had shaved; there was something sinister about the intense look in his eyes. When he accepted the lit cigarette I handed him and started to light his own with it, I caught a glimpse of the tattoo under the cuff of his shirtsleeve. As he tried to give me back my cigarette after lighting up, he dropped it at my feet.

"Uh-oh. Sorry about that."

He looked at my face as he spoke. The whites of his eyes were bloodshot, but his dark pupils were steady, fixed, as though stabbing me. He pulled a crumpled ten-thousand-yen note from his pants pocket and stuffed it into the breast pocket of my jacket.

"Here, take this and buy yourself some smokes."

No sooner had he said this than he walked off, a lean figure without an umbrella in the rain. I made an impatient noise through my teeth as I watched him go.

I was about to visit somebody I had never met. A complete stranger. My only hope was to talk this stranger into giving me a job so that I could keep on living. I had lost everything, thrown everything away. I had already been made to understand, all too well, that I was a loser. Whoever I was about to meet was probably used to being tough toward people as unworldly as me. No matter; whether it turned out to be some guy I couldn't get anywhere with, or a woman with a heart of stone, I had no other choice; I was at the end of my rope.

I couldn't afford to dwell on my regrets at this point. In my apartment in Tokyo, I had nightly dreams about running around with the clothes on my back on fire and throwing myself off a cliff. No, it was nothing more than me just clinging to my own incompetence. With the help of a hand-drawn map, I found my way to the Igaya. This was a *yakitori* grill in the Higashi-Naniwachō district, the kind you can find anywhere. There was a big mirror on the wall to one side of the shop. A smell like meat juices gone bad came drifting out of the back, where there was no sign of human activity. It was afternoon on the second day of a two-day holiday in February. A chill rose up from around my feet. I was tense from an anxiety that seemed to be forcing all my blood downward. A thin-haired woman, pushing sixty, came out to meet me. When I introduced myself, she said, "So you're the one, huh?" with a sour expression. She proceeded to look me over, then sat down without inviting me to do the same. I'm sure you can't run a small business like this in a charitable spirit, at least when it comes to money, any more than you can any other. She dragged an ashtray on the table toward her with a matchstick, then lit a cigarette. Her hands were wrinkled from a life of working to survive.

"Kanida-san says you've got a college degree."

I said nothing.

"He said it was a fancy school, too. Isn't that right?"

"Well, yes . . . "

"Yes, hell, you shameless scum."

Anywhere I go this is how the conversation usually starts. This woman was the first ever to call me a shameless scum so clearly to my face, however.

"Oh, never mind. There's always some that get dealt a good hand and go bust anyway."

I understood her anger very well. No doubt I did look like a gutless, spiritless worm. She wanted to say, *Look at you, poor thing—while everybody else in this world is scrambling after money.* That was what my mother said to me when I came crawling back to the family home in Banshū-Shikama, west of Kobe, after I went bust in Tokyo. I knew then in my heart there was no place left for me to run.

But I didn't care; let someone call me names, even "shameless scum." I didn't care, but my ass was oozing oil every day. I was disgusted with being myself. Hating what made me who I am was like being in a quarrel. In a quarrel, the essence of either opponent's personality inevitably surfaces. Maybe I didn't care because gradually wasting away to my own essence was making me content in some way. I was also physically wasting away in the process, however; no wonder my ass was oozing oil.

I wanted somehow to find words that would resolve my status as an ex-white-collar worker—no, it was practically impossible; what I really wanted was to hear words that would rewrite my entire spiritual history for me. I was pleading in my heart for it; my mind had lost all sense of purpose.

I had done some reading in college. I read Nietzsche and Kafka, looking words up in a German dictionary as I went. Then again, I read the folklorist Orikuchi Shinobu; I read Maruyama Masao, the political philosopher. The result, I suppose, was that I became one of those that "get dealt a good hand and go bust anyway." Otherwise, there's no way I would have quit my job without having any prospects for the future. There were other unavoidable issues in the run-up to my resignation, of course, but it's all more or less sound and fury now.

After I quit, I fooled around aimlessly for two and a half years until I ended up with absolutely nothing left to my name. In other words, I slid into both economic and spiritual bankruptcy while wasting time in a state of total indecision. Anybody will look for ways out when in trouble, but once in that kind of situation there's no hope of escape. After all, I had no clear idea which way to look for words that could transform my spiritual history. I had no idea whether seeking such a transformation would resurrect my being, or if I would end up trapped someplace in an even more agonizing state than I was in now. While these two possibilities were constantly, vaguely tangling in my mind, I was sure of one thing: it was unbearably painful to be who I was.

I wanted to know what this sparse-haired woman in front of me was really like. She spoke to me again, looking at me with eyes like soup left over in the bottom of a bowl, repeatedly clicking her teeth. "Kanida-san told me it didn't matter how much it was as long as I just paid you something, but I want you to tell me: how much do you want?"

I had no idea what it would be like with a woman almost sixty, but it suddenly occurred to me that I wouldn't mind making love to her. Any woman's worth sleeping with at least once. Having no idea that I was thinking such thoughts, of course, she went on. I think she said "I want you to fix me a thousand skewers of *yakitori* a day, at three yen apiece." At least that's what she was saying out loud, but like me she gave no sign of what might actually be going through her head. That's the normal situation between human beings: it's the human condition.

"Come on, now. How much?"

"The more the better with money, isn't it—even just one yen?"

"You mean you don't like my offer?"

I didn't answer.

"I want you to be satisfied with your job." She looked at me coldly. "Oh, by the way: what's your name?"

"Ikushima Yoichi."

"Well. Your parents gave you a nice name, didn't they?" Her tone was sarcastic.

"Your offer's fine with me."

"Good."

She looked pleased. It was going to be this way all along,

anyway. I had come to earn money, to be sure, but hadn't intended to really *make* money; I was unable to resolve that contradiction, so couldn't explain it to anyone else. It was best, then, to say nothing more about it. It made no difference, for instance, that I didn't know the name of this woman who owned the Igaya. All I cared to know was what she really was; if I didn't find that out, though, that's all there would be to it.

From Higashi-Naniwachō the owner of the Igaya took me to the Deyashiki district, where there was a cluster of big markets: Sanwa Market, Nice Market, New Sanwa, and so on. Under the great steel-framed roofs hundreds of stalls were lined up, each with its sign, selling a vast array of things: meat, poultry, fish, vegetables, fruit, tofu, salted and dried foodstuffs, all piled up in heaps. Business seemed to be good; the whole market district was bustling. Just a short way from all this activity, however, the scene changed abruptly to rows of shabby houses. Near Deyashiki Station was a stretch of cheap drinking joints, reeking of soy sauce and charred garlic, and flophouses catering to homeless drifters.

On a back street in this quarter was a store that carried general merchandise, stuff like soap and rubber gloves. After stopping in briefly to exchange greetings there, my new employer went down a side alley and walked up to the second floor of a dilapidated, grimy, wood-framed apartment house. There were three units on either side of a central corridor, but the place had a lifeless, deserted air. Without having to unlock the door, she entered the last apartment on the right. A peculiar odor stung my nostrils. It was that same smell: like spoiled meat juices. The interior consisted of a single, barren four-and-a-half-mat room with a sink and a window. A rather large electric refrigerator incongruously occupied one corner, with a shabby wooden chair next to it. There was nothing else. A neighboring house backed right up to the window, making it half dark, so that it would have been hard to read a newspaper even during the day. However, I could see clearly that the straw tatami mats on the floor were oddly discolored from age. The cold crept up from my feet and traveled through my whole body. Switching on the shaded hanging lightbulb, the woman started explaining how, starting tomorrow, she expected me to handle pig and cattle organs. Then she made an abrupt remark.

"Oh, I want to be straight with you about something." She suddenly grabbed my hand. "You're cute."

Instantly, I pulled my hand back. A shiver went up my spine. She had sensed what I had been thinking back at the shop in Higashi-Naniwachō. *Creepy, lecherous old bag*, you might think, but the idea must have been welcome to this woman in her late fifties. She gave a loud, offhand laugh.

"Ah, ha, ha . . . you're such a straight arrow it's disgusting."

Like the point of a pushpin, those words "straight arrow" stabbed me to the heart. That offhand laugh must have been a sign; I had hurt her so much she couldn't help herself.

Night came. I pulled the padded futon bedding out of the closet and burrowed into it. It stank; there was no telling who else had slept under these musty-smelling covers. Some stranger's hair oil had seeped into the pillowcase. The room had no heating device. Other than the refrigerator and the wooden chair, there was nothing in it but a cutting board, a cleaver, a small sharp-pointed knife, and some bamboo skewers stored under the sink. I was thankful, however, since the room and bedding were free and I had no other way of making a living. The futon was cold, but I felt no desire to sleep someplace warm.

I had slept under just such cold covers in a cheap apartment when I had my office job. My position in the company was in ad marketing. People like me were a dime a dozen; it was just an ordinary white-collar job, for what it was worth, but sometimes it got mistakenly played up as a glamorous, cutting-edge occupation. Quite a few people threw themselves into the work and devoted their entire lives to it. Obsessive as I was, however, I felt a certain element missing, something that should have made the daily grind of selling advertising worthwhile. My attitude seemed arrogant, not to say absurd, even to me; others went so far as to criticize me for outrageous presumption.

Amid the day-to-day routine of selling ads I had an uneasy feeling, as if my individuality were somehow being washed away. Not that I actually had any well-defined sense of self: I might have thought of some given "I" as the one and only "I," yet that "I" was only what had been created by its relationship to others, given form by inhaling others' fabricated opinions, ultimately a vague "I" with no definition of how closely it might represent my true nature. It made me uneasy to see even that sort of self being washed away, yet behind this uneasiness lurked an odious "I" that considered this very uneasiness a burden. It was unbearable to me to be myself; at the same time, my self was being pointlessly washed away.

As I sat alone in my apartment at night, an indefinable fear of living would arise in me. It was as though I had been possessed by a *mono no ke*—one of those evil spirits of legend. I was completely laid bare. Along with the loss of what is important and necessary, being washed away also means the falling away of unnecessary things and the gradual wasting away of the self toward the core of one's nature. My fear of living was growing more and more intense. I finally began having dreams where I ran around with my back on fire.

Life was stable in spite of all that, for what it was worth, with a steady monthly income to support me. Under the influence of that *mono no ke*, I grew uncomfortable leading the same steady lifestyle; it began to seem inexcusable. I was overcome by a desire to shatter that stability all of a sudden.

Take the following incident that took place in a department store one day. I was suddenly seized with an impulse to murder the girl who was wrapping up a pair of scissors I had just bought. She was attractive enough to look at, but her color seemed somehow unhealthy. When she asked me, "Is something wrong?" I was stymied. It was not as though she had wrapped the package carelessly or had been rude in handing it to me. A distinct, unsettling cold sensation emanating from this girl had aroused a pain that I had been suppressing; I began to feel a desire to suddenly hurl both her and myself into the pit of hell. It was an irrational, insane desire. I was terrified of the *mono no ke* within me, yet there was no longer anything I could do about this raw urge that had reared up in my mind. *Go ahead and die!* I thought to myself. Rather than kill this sick-looking young woman, however, I threw myself off the cliff.

Was this a sign that I wanted to sleep someplace warm? Actually, from this point on I began to sleep under even colder covers. I felt a certain perverse comfort in doing so, but there was nothing more to the comfort than that it existed. I grew afraid of becoming caught on the jagged obstacles along the bottom, beneath the currents of my consciousness. I had not a speck of regret about breaking up the elements of my stable life, but an irritating feeling that somehow it was not enough, that I could not keep it up, continued to gnaw at me little by little. It puzzled me. I had tried breaking out of my settled lifestyle, but it was making no difference. The ominous fear of living that had possessed me still haunted me within, making some sort of unfathomable appeal. I had no desire to start on any new course of action. I couldn't accept the idea of my life going nowhere, but I thought it would do just that, and didn't find the prospect particularly distressing.

Some people in this world find their sense of purpose in life in continual prayer for the soul of someone they've killed. A different world might have opened up for me if I'd given in to the impulse then and there and killed that woman with those scissors. But it was all a nightmare to me. It was in the darkness of the decrepit apartment house in Deyashiki that I awoke from the nightmare.

The owner of the Igaya had grasped my hand, and the feel of it was still fresh in my memory. It was a lonely, cold hand. My hearing grew spontaneously keener. I had been hearing children's voices and other noises downstairs until just a little while ago, but now it had stopped; there was no sign of any activity in the other units on the second floor. I got up and walked out into the corridor. No trace of light leaked from the other rooms. I went to the toilet at the top of the stairs. It had no urinal, only a compartment with a squat-type fixture in the floor. As I crouched over it, I saw in front of my eyes a drawing scratched into the wall in jerky lines with something like a nail. It was of a wide-eyed woman with a man's thick penis in her mouth.

I woke up the next morning when a young man came bursting through the door. He wore a baseball cap and was carrying a large plastic bag. His eyes were piercingly sharp. The bag sagged shapelessly as he dropped it with a thud on the floor by the entry. I could tell that it contained things like pork and beef organs and plucked chicken flesh. Looking at his face, I was about to speak but then stopped and said nothing, since he wouldn't take his eyes off me. Just by his look, his eyes seemed to be transmitting some sort of evil. He turned his back and left, again hitting the door with a bang. A few moments later, the noise of a car engine sounded in front of the variety store and then faded away.

I cleaned up, got dressed, and went outside. Finding a public telephone, I called the Igaya and reported what had happened. The owner answered, "Really? I'll be right there." I got a croquette at the candy shop and had them fry it up; I was waiting in the apartment eating it when she arrived. She immediately began explaining to me with great care how to carve up the organ meat and put the pieces on skewers. "Now, see this yellow fat? You need to cut it off." "Here's how you cut the tendons." True to her feminine nature, she was very particular about things. "Oh, that was Sai-chan. He'll be bringing you the stuff every day," was all she would say about the man who had come by earlier, nothing more. *Who's that guy work for? What's the arrangement for his bringing the stuff? Why didn't he ask me to sign any sort of receipt when he delivered it?* Most of all I'd been wondering since she brought me here, *why work in this apartment instead of in the kitchen at her place?* She gave me no chance to ask any of the questions on my mind. No doubt there was some reason, whatever it might be, for going to the trouble of processing the meat in an apartment like this. But the impression she gave was that there was no need for me to know.

Having gone through her list of instructions, she said to me, "Oh, you know what? I haven't even offered you a cup of tea yet. I'm sorry. You drink coffee?"

"Coffee? Well, actually, I . . . "

"Oh, come on. Do me a favor and come have one with me."

I stayed silent.

"I remembered late last night. I should have known better."

She had been thinking about me in bed last night, rubbing her cold hands together, while I was struggling for peace of mind.

We went to a coffee shop called Ringoya in front of Deyashiki Station. As we opened the door to go in, a young woman who was paying her bill suddenly called out, "Oh, auntie! Thank you so much for what you did the other day!"

The two of them then started a conversation that I couldn't follow. In between things like "My older brother sent another letter" and "I was sure, after I'd asked Shirai-san in Hiroshima to . . . " the young woman, naturally, glanced at me from time to time. I glanced back. She was so good-looking that it hurt to look at her. Her eyes glittered like a bird of prey's. I looked away.

But as I pretended to look elsewhere, I checked her out from head to toe. Catching on quickly, she made a move with her right hand as if to cover herself in front; after looking back at me once more, she cast down her eyes. When her eyes turned downward, her face betrayed a dark something that she seemed to be hiding. The proprietress of the Igaya shot me a sharp look out of the corner of her eye. I turned my face away, but at the same moment I stole another glance at the young woman. I couldn't help it; she was that beautiful. Her black hair shimmered in the light.

The two finished their conversation. Taking one last look at me, the young woman left. The older one and I found seats in the back of the shop and sat down. She ordered two coffees.

Although we were now sitting face to face, she didn't speak. She sat there with her head a little bowed as if caught up in thought, chewing her nails, looking toward me from time to time with a harsh look in her eyes. The coffee arrived, but still she said nothing while we stirred the cups with our spoons. It was becoming hard for me to bear, but for that very reason I was determined not to say anything. The first one to speak would self-destruct.

"How old were you when the war ended?"

"I was born in the afternoon on the day before the big air raid is what I heard."

"Let's see—that means you were born in the year of the rooster, and you're thirty-three."

"I suppose so."

"I was twenty-seven at the end of the war."

"I see."

"I was living in Kishiwada then. I went straight to Osaka and started picking up GI's in the occupation forces—a hooker, a *pan-pan*, at my age."

Inwardly, I gasped.

"What you looking like that for? You never heard of a hooker?"

"Well, actually—"

I remembered the cold touch of her hands.

"I went home to my daddy in Kishiwada with the money I got from the GI's—*Amerika-san*, we called 'em—wearing my red high heels. Yeah, high heels some GI bought for me. And you know what he said?"

I had no response.

"'Nice shoes.' That's all he said."

I couldn't understand what this woman was trying to get across, but one thing was clear: no part of her life was more difficult to talk about, and she was talking about it.

"I thought about it on my way back to the shop from your

apartment yesterday and decided I had to tell you this story, no matter what."

"Pardon?"

"According to Kanida-san, you graduated from a top school and had a job with a good company. And then you went and said to hell with it."

I didn't know what old Kanida had told this woman, or how he said it, but it seemed as though she might be making some kind of mistake about me. Whatever one might make of the confusion in my mind, all I saw from a very candid and factual review of my experiences was that I had gradually ruined myself, even been abandoned by a woman, while living a feckless life with no future.

"Before today, I've never told anybody that I was ever a *panpan*. I've hidden it all along. Some people know about it anyway, but I always wanted to tell somebody about it myself just once, from my own lips, before I died. It's hard living with a secret."

"Ah. I see . . . "

"Life in this world's tough, right? That's exactly why people ought to keep in mind that everybody needs a break. But you know, everybody's always rushing like a bat out of hell to cut off the next guy, even when they're only getting on the Hanshin train. What I'm saying is, living means giving things up. You gave everything up, yourself. I gave myself up, too—sacrificed myself—when I decided to be a whore."

For this woman, having been a prostitute in her youth was a loathsome past, or at least she spoke of it in that tone. In a book I once read, I saw the Chinese characters for "prostitute" written with the phonetic syllables *jigoku*—"hell." With those blood-stained words—"red high heels"—she was confessing a past spent in hell.

Words suddenly began to attack me: the disappointments she must have felt; the sorrows; the resentment—but there's a morbid pleasure in confession. How was I to accept this? Why had she decided to tell me this story? I was no saint, much less the Judge of Hell; to put it bluntly, I was nothing but a loser. As she made her confession to me, the unapologetic pleasure she seemed to be feeling cut into my being like the touch of her icy hands.

"Ikushima-han, you're just a kid. At your age, you ought to be getting a lot dirtier—well, I say that, but you're not up to it."

I felt faintly humiliated. Still, why had this woman felt compelled to tell me that she had been a prostitute?

"That Aya-chan you saw a while ago—she's pretty good-looking, right?"

"Well, yes."

"You don't have to look so shook up, either."

" . . ."

"I want you to know something. That girl's Korean."

I felt another shock of recognition. My parents had spoken privately in the same tone about the Koreans who lived on the outskirts of our village. Some people in my generation who caught that contagion still talk about them in the same contemptuous way. I couldn't say that I hadn't contracted some of the same attitude myself. My shock of recognition came from that realization. There was a deeper meaning in the way the owner of the Igaya was talking to me, however. She had put her finger squarely on the fascination I had felt when I saw that girl. There was something seething in this old woman that could not go without being said. Was it because that girl radiated such sensuousness that no man could resist staring at her? But why was it impossible to resist?

3

I stayed holed up in my room every day, cutting up beef and pork organs and dissecting poultry, impaling the meat on skewers. Not being used to the work, I frequently misjudged the force I needed and ended up skewering my own fingers. All of it being the flesh of dead animals, the fat that stuck to my hands reeked of blood. I found myself sometimes recalling songs that I had learned in childhood, like the one a priest used to sing for me when he came to perform the Buddhist rites on my ancestors' death anniversaries: *There's a tree in the garden, a jujube tree . . .*

Sai-chan came regularly at ten in the morning and five in the evening, bringing the big plastic bag and picking up the finished work. He never said anything; as always, he just looked at me with those savage eyes. I thought about trying to draw him out but decided there was no use in it, figuring there was some significance to his silence.

It was nine or ten at night by the time I finished a day's work. The second floor of the apartment building was very still at that hour, just as it had been on the first night I arrived here. Gradually I realized that a man occasionally went in and out of the room across the hall and that a couple of fairly advanced age came home to the apartment next door usually late at night. By the sounds that came through the wall, I could tell they were sometimes quite drunk; I could even hear the uninhibited noises of lovemaking. I had not yet seen the man, but when I ran into the woman coming out of the shared toilet early one morning I could see that she was pathologically fat and well past her prime in looks. In age she was probably not far from the owner of the Igaya. During the daytime there was no sign of activity next door.

A number of men visited the room across the hall during the day. One of them would come thudding up the steps and bang rudely on the door, shouting, "Hey, Doc, you home?" From the sinister sound of his voice and the manner of his walk, I sensed that he could not be in any conventional line of work. Stepping into the corridor one afternoon, I came face-to-face with a man; I was surprised to see that it was the pale, shifty-eyed character who had thrust the ten-thousand-yen note into my breast pocket on my first day in town. He only glanced at my face for a moment, however, then went on into the apartment. If he had recognized me, he gave no indication of it. When I came back from my errand feeling rather uneasy and was about to enter my room, I heard a peculiar groan in a male voice coming out of the apartment across the hall. I listened and heard it again, a sound like someone enduring intense pain. It was followed by a threatening command: "Damn it, shut up."

But there was another groan that sounded even more agonized than before, as if bursting out of someone's guts despite his efforts to hold it in. I wondered if this was some sort of gangland torture session. I listened intently for what was going on in the unit across the hall as I processed the animal parts in my own room, but there was no sign of anything more. When I cracked the door slightly and looked out, all I heard were those same intermittent groans. As darkness eventually began to fall, I heard a door open and a man call out, "Thanks, Doc!" as he hurried off. There was silence after that, and then someone else went out. I was sure it was the one with that pallid face.

I heard the same visitor's voice the next day as he arrived and went into the apartment across the hall. Once again, he emitted the same groans, then left with the same parting remark. That evening when I went downstairs after Sai-chan left, I abruptly came face-to-face on the bottom landing with a young woman who had just come in from outside. She looked startled. She was the one I had met the other day at the Ringoya. Just like the time before, she didn't take her eyes off me. After fixing me with that glare, she walked on down the corridor. Reaching the unit on the right side at the far end, the one directly beneath mine, she took out her key and opened the door. Just as she was about to enter the room, she turned and glanced in my direction. Our eyes met, and I felt a brief shock. I got the uneasy feeling that it wasn't good for me for her to know that I had been following her with my eyes.

After that evening, I began to listen for the noises and the sound of a child's voice originating from the unit beneath mine. It was a little boy's voice; sometimes, I could hear him singing.

As the days passed, I couldn't help beginning to notice the activities of the people living reclusively in this old tenement building. Downstairs, there was a middle-aged woman with some kind of job and an old couple who seemed to have no discernible means of support. I occasionally saw men of indeterminate character coming and going. They were bound to notice me, too, of course. I might be trying to hide from society, but as eye contact grew more frequent when we passed by on stair landings and in other places, it became natural at least to give a quick nod; in fact, forces were at work that made it unavoidable. From even such slight contacts I began to draw definite conclusions about their personalities and, inevitably, to understand them without ever exchanging a word.

I quickly recognized the small boy whose voice I was hearing from downstairs. He looked to be about in first grade; he had fine features, but there was a somber look in his eyes that didn't seem right for a child. I saw him for the first time as he was coming home from school, wearing his backpack. That was all there was to it then, but the next time I saw him he was playing by himself in the alley next to the building, drawing some kind of picture on the pavement. As I walked by, he looked up at me and said, "Don't step on it!"

Looking at him closely for the first time then, I was sure that he was the child whose voice I could hear coming from downstairs. I couldn't imagine that young woman being his mother, however; nor could I picture her as his sister.

One night, as I was buying a can of saké from a vending machine on my way home from the public baths, I heard a voice calling out to me from behind: "Hey, handsome, wanna go somewhere and have a good time?"

I turned around and saw one of the streetwalkers who loitered in the shadows on corners around this district at night, trolling for men. Not only that: on closer inspection in the dim light, I could see that it was the woman next door. She evidently realized it, too; she made a sharp chucking sound through her teeth and glared at me, but didn't turn away. As I stood staring at her, she said, "What the hell you looking at?" and came toward me. Quickly sensing a threat, I dodged her and walked back to my apartment as fast as I could. She didn't come back to the room next door that night. There had been other nights when no sound came from that room. The next night, I heard the door open fairly early; there was the boisterous sound of a man and woman's voices, and then they left. Much later, someone came back again; the voices I overheard didn't seem to belong to the same couple I had heard before.

The same sort of thing went on for three or four days. One night, I went out deliberately into the hall when I sensed someone leaving and found a couple I had never seen standing there. The woman glanced at me; so did the man, but he immediately looked away. The room next door was being rented by streetwalkers as a place to bring their johns.

After I began paying more attention, I confirmed that it was actually not one woman, but two or three, taking turns bringing in men, as I had suspected from listening. None of these women was a day under fifty, with straggly hair beginning to grow thin; their customers, too, were all shabby older men that looked like homeless laborer types. Sometimes a couple wouldn't make a sound after tumbling into bed together amid peals of laughter, and then later I would begin hearing a strange, drawn-out chant muttered in an unknown tongue. It might have been some sort of magic spell or religious formula; there was no way to know. If these women were pitiable, so were the men. The bizarre sound of their voices could not but strike to the very core of a listener's soul.

The owner of the Igaya, the one they called Seiko Nēsan—"Big Sister Seiko"—was no doubt all too familiar with the desperate, tragic little dramas that played themselves out in the darkness. I was sure that she had made her devastating confession to me with full knowledge that I would be hearing such things one day. Back then, it was "red high heels"; now it was incantations uttered by some aging prostitute in search of solace. Nonetheless her sudden revelation to me was working like venom in my brain.

Seiko Nēsan dropped by my room occasionally, saying that she was on her way home from shopping at the markets; she always brought some sweets or fruit. At those times, she sat in my unheated room and watched how I worked. She generally ate one of the tangerines she had brought, smoked a cigarette, and left; I would stay resolutely silent all the while, and she too would say little more than maybe "You been drinking this much every night, huh?" as she looked at the row of saké bottles I had bought out of the vending machines and finished off. As she looked at the empties she knew full well, of course, that I couldn't go drinking in the bars on the kind of money I made there. She never invited me to come have a drink at the Igaya, though, and I wouldn't have felt like doing it.

Even so, for some reason the woman was buying sweets and fruit for me. I would have been more grateful if she had brought a thermos of tea or something, actually, but there was no way in the world I could say that. Seiko Nēsan was well aware that there was no convenient appliance like that in my room.

Each time after she left, I found cigarette butts crushed into the peelings of the tangerine she had eaten. Sometimes there was lipstick on the ends, and I left the remains just as they were until her next visit. She would notice it the next time, of course, but not say a word as the smoke from her cigarette floated away in the air. She was probably thinking that I had some nerve. I was thinking the same thing about her as I chopped up the organ meat or stuck the chopped pieces on the skewers.

There was nothing more to those brief moments, but in that bleak room it was comforting in its own way to sit with Seiko Nēsan during her visits. I itched to question her about why she hadn't mentioned the groans of the men from across the hall or told me that the girl we had met at the Ringoya was living in the apartment below mine, but it would have been prying to ask such questions. Just as Sai-chan never said anything, it was clear to me that she, too, had plenty of reasons to stay silent. At the same time, I had been given mental custody of her loath-some past, something that had already invaded my conscious-ness several times as I listened to the old whore's eerie chanting in the room next door.

4

It was just after the middle of March. I went to the post office to buy postcards, and while I was there I ran into that pallid-faced man. I offered a polite glance, but he showed no sign of a response. I decided that he must have forgotten me. There was a small boy with him, maybe a first-grader; nudging the child in the head, he said, "Let's go," and they left the post office. As they were leaving, I felt a slight shock of recognition when I saw the boy's face from the side. He was the one I'd seen from time to time, playing by himself in the alley by the apartment building. From the way the man had nudged the boy's head as they left, just then they seemed—no matter how you looked at it—like father and son. Who was that young woman, then? I had already seen the boy once, in the corridor, addressing her as "Aya-chan" in a tone suggesting she was not his mother. At least it was certain that she and this boy were living in the apartment directly beneath mine. I wondered if all this meant the man was sharing the apartment with them.

Judging from their looks, the men who came and went across the hall clearly belonged to the kind called *kusubori* or "burn-outs," the name given around here to the petty hoodlums who smoldered in the dark depths of society. I remember, when I was working in that cheap eatery in Kobe, hearing the toughs who came into shop say things like "You know, us *kusubori* . . . "; it may have been a somewhat self-deprecating way of speech among them, but I don't think the term counted as an insult. Every time one of them came pounding up the stairs to visit the pale man in the apartment across the hall, I heard groans of bullet-biting agony. It seemed as if their whole reason for coming was to suffer.

One evening a few days later when I went to the public baths, I found the place empty except for two or three other customers. As I was soaking in the hot pool after washing off, another man approached. He was middle-aged and strongly built. I was startled when I got a glimpse of his back: it was completely covered with a tattooed design of the demonic blue-skinned god Fudō, surrounded by butterflies wildly fluttering among crimson flames. When I saw this, it dawned on me what must have been causing those groans in the apartment across the hall. As I thought about it, it all fell into place: the men who came to see the pale-faced man and called him "Doc"; the voices that sometimes went on all night. Hadn't I already seen the tattoos on his own wrist at the Amagasaki train station, that first day I met him?

In any case, it amazed me to think what a strange force a tattoo could exert. The demon-god covering the back of this man now sitting in the bathing pool right in front of me gave off a terrifying glow. It was unbearable to look at. Why was that? The tattoo was somehow fundamentally different from the painted images of this deity in Buddhist religious art. I wondered what it was about this image that could arouse such fear that I found it impossible to look at directly.

After coming home from the baths that night, I took out the postcards I had bought. As though possessed by the glistening evil I had seen at the bathhouse just a short while before, I wanted to write something to somebody, anybody. When I started to write, however, I realized that I had no one to address my message to. It had been only a little over three years since I abandoned my life in Tokyo, but in the space of those three years plus I had lost all connections of that sort. If I wrote about my life for what it really was, it would come across to the recipient as nothing more than a selfish complaint.

I'm so tired of your whining.

Hell, I thought you were living like that because you wanted it that way.

I had already received more than a couple of letters in that vein. I suppose it meant that those were the kind of people I used to associate with.

I had gone to buy those postcards in spite of all that. I just wanted to write to somebody. The plain truth is that I wanted to cry on somebody's shoulder. I wrote a name and address on the front of one card after another, but couldn't write a thing on the other side of any of them. One after another, they went into the trash; when the ten cards I'd bought at the post office were all gone, the peace that comes with silence descended on me. Maybe I had gone to the post office to buy the cards because I wanted to attain this state of peace. No doubt I'd go there again to buy postcards, stamps, or whatever, thinking all the while about the despairing sound of that old prostitute's chanting in the next room.

One afternoon when I went out into the corridor, I could hear men talking in low voices in the apartment across the hall. I continued to the common toilet on the second floor. Just as I was about to pull the door open, Aya-chan came out, startling me. She only shot me a glance, however, then went on down the corridor. As she got to my door, she turned around to look at me again before going into the apartment across the way. As I straddled the toilet, the drawing of the woman with the penis in her mouth was again right in front of me. Moments before, Aya-chan had been looking at this drawing as well while straddling this fixture. I had no doubt that the hint of a smile in her eyes as she glanced back at me was connected to the memory of that drawing.

"You son of a bitch, I oughta kill you!" Sai-chan shouted at me unexpectedly one evening.

I was bewildered. He came up onto the tatami floor in his street shoes and acted as though he was about to grab me by the front of my shirt. It was surprising that he had spoken at all, and it terrified me not to know what I had done to provoke his anger. I was just about to hand him the pile of meat I had prepared, as usual, since that was what he'd come for. He seemed to have gained some sort of satisfaction, though, just from shouting at me and seeing how fearful I was; he took the meat and left without making any further move toward me. Maybe I had been somehow careless. Usually Sai-chan never said a thing, so all I ever did was just hand him the meat, also without a word. Maybe I had become too used to the situation and begun to take it for granted. Something must have rubbed him the wrong way, but try as I might, I couldn't come up with a reason. It left me feeling insecure and uncomfortable.

The next day, I felt strangely tense as I waited for Sai-chan to arrive, but he just took the meat from me in the usual way and left, acting as if he'd never torn into me the day before. The anxiety he stirred in me did not go away readily, however.

It's not easy to fathom what fearsome things lurk in the human mind. This was true not only of Sai-chan, but of practically everyone else I knew; because of it, I hadn't the slightest intention of mentioning Sai-chan's shouting at me to the mistress of the Igaya, who had made that painful confession to me. Seiko Nēsan continued to come once or twice a week and silently blow cigarette smoke into the air. I had no idea what she thought or felt while she was there doing that. Maybe she, too, had some sad incantation in her mind as she came to the apartment, but there was no justification for me to pry into such things. Sai-chan probably hadn't said anything to her either; it was odd to be so sure about something like that, but for me the evidence in his eyes was convincing.

5

On days off, after washing my clothes I had nothing else left to do. One day, I went out to eat lunch in the neighborhood and took a walk along the central shopping arcade in downtown Amagasaki. The shops that lined both sides of the street had attractive displays of merchandise to catch the eye, but there was nothing I wanted in any of their show windows. Not that the goods didn't look well made; if I'd been the same person I was several years before, I would have wanted plenty of things that were on display there. Now, however, I had no desire for anything more than the absolute minimum needed to survive. Looking into the window displays gradually became disgusting; I had the uneasy feeling that I was beating myself senseless by degrees.

Eventually I arrived in front of the Hanshin Railway Amaga-saki Station. It was a bright, clear day in April. Seeing a crowd in one corner of the station plaza, I went closer and saw a huckster with a blue-green snake wrapped around his neck, busily spouting his pitch. It was a scene I had often witnessed on shrine festival days as a child; I had fond memories of it, but it also made me uncomfortable: not just the unfounded disquiet that comes from seeing a reptile, but also the peculiar nostalgia I felt from seeing a snake handler in action.

The look in the snake handler's eyes was serious, even vicious. I had a brief, oppressive feeling that this strapping hustler was probably not making this kind of living of his own will; when I was a child, a thought like that would never have crossed my mind. I was peeking at this scene from behind the backs of the crowd, however, just as I had been peeking into the show windows, out of an insatiable desire somewhere within.

I went to the prefectural library in downtown Osaka that day. Seeing the snake handler had reminded me of a horrifying novel by Heine that I had read while in school, called *Les Dieux en Exil*, and I wanted to read it again. While the girl at the desk was gone looking for the book in the stacks, I picked up a few books that had been left on a rack right in front of me; a poem called "Too Late" jumped out at me.

> *That hat*
> *Was swallowed by a wave*
> *In an instant, as I stumbled.*
> *Please pick it up it for me.*
> *It's drifting on the waves.*
> *See, look:*
> *It's just within reach.*
> *I know you've tried to reach out to it*
> *As hard as you could.*
> *The ocean's waters are angry today;*
> *The waves are trying to swallow even you.*
> *But please don't be afraid,*
> *And get that hat for me.*

It was in an anthology called *Roses of Light* by a woman named Shindō Ryōko. I had no idea what kind of person she was, but I felt as if I had swallowed some sort of frightening words—frightening the same way Seiko Nēsan's were when she told me *picking up GI's in the occupation forces—a hooker, a pan-pan at my . . . .* Just then, the girl librarian came back and told me that the book I was looking for wasn't available. She wore glasses. In the brief time she had been wandering around the stacks, I had been ambushed by those words: *But getting the hat back/ Wasn't what I really wanted.* I remembered the icy touch of Seiko Nēsan's hand.

The cherry trees were in full bloom outside the library. The poem was in a volume with a scarlet binding. I decided to copy it in my notebook before I left. As I copied the words one by one, feeling chilled to the bone, I was reminded of a college friend.

He had gone to work in the research department of a bank after graduation; when I saw him a few years later, he was already married. There was nothing remarkable about that in itself, but I learned that he was in the habit of getting up every morning while his wife was still asleep, doing the laundry, and copying Buddhist scriptures before leaving for work. He responded to my puzzled inquiry with an expression of pleasure; he said that his wife was the kind of woman who wrote poetry and translated mystery novels. He told me that his wife would deliberately soil her panties at least once during her period every month, and he had begun copying scriptures to calm his feelings while washing out her blood-soaked underwear whenever that time of month came around.

For a woman who writes poetry, and has an insatiable desire for fulfillment, I suppose there was no other choice for keeping alive the freshness of married life as it eroded day by day. No doubt by the same token, once she began acting like that, he had to do something like copying the words of Buddha every day to achieve some peace of mind. Still, it was somehow disgusting to hear him spill the contents of their love life in such a smug manner.

My morose copying of some unknown woman's poetry into a notebook was certainly a depraved kind of act, too, and not so very different. Why did I throw those ten postcards into the trash the other night? What kind of peace had I found by keeping silence that evening? More to the point: what does it mean to write? What sort of thing is it to write poetry? Why did that woman find it imperative to soil her underwear deliberately each time her period came? But no—why, of all things, was I feeling driven to copy this poem "Too Late" into my notebook? I recited it once again, to myself, by heart; then I violently shredded the page I had copied it on, threw it away, and left the library. An indefinable sense of humiliation sent a chill through my mind.

On a different day, as I was walking down a road along the Hanshin Railway tracks, I saw a man squatting on his haunches in the courtyard of a Shinto shrine. It was the one with the unhealthy complexion who lived in my apartment building. Without moving from that position, he was throwing stones at some of the free-roaming chickens that were kept at the shrine. At first glance he seemed to be doing this just to pass the time, but after a closer look I realized that he never missed: every time, he hit a chicken's eye. Whenever a chicken was hit, it jumped into the air. That wasn't all. Next he threw what looked like a razor blade, and when it found its mark in the chicken's eye the bird gave a piercing screech and ran off.

Several days later, while I was eating at a cheap restaurant in the neighborhood, the woman running the place asked me:

"Say, aren't you the gentleman who lives over there in the same place as Horimayu-san the tattooist?" She was a chatterbox. She went on, "He's a scary man. Don't you think so? He sticks people with a needle, thousands of times, and it doesn't bother him a bit."

To hear her go on, I thought she might know something about the animal guts and raw chicken I was skewering, but I was afraid if I said something to such a loose-lipped woman, it might just backfire on me, so I decided to stay quiet.

Once cherry blossom season was over, warm breezes followed the sunshine and the color of the budding new leaves grew brighter by the day. Now and then, the weather would turn for the worse; as the air grew chilly again, the lightning that came with the spring thunderstorms flashed across my lap as I sat. I had apparently caught a cold; I had an unpleasant cough that lasted day after day. But Sai-chan came twice a day, regular as clockwork, so I couldn't very well take any time off.

"Mayu-san! Hey! Mayu-san!" I heard a deep male voice calling out as someone rapped on the door across the hall one day. There seemed to be no answer, however. Suddenly, the door of my apartment was jerked open. A man who looked about the same age as me was standing there; I could tell with one look that he was a hoodlum.

"My name's Sanada. Sorry to bother you, but could you ask Ayako downstairs to call me when she gets back?"

"Sure."

"What's your name?"

"Ikushima. But—"

"All right, then. Sorry about that, but I'll count on you."

That night, when I knocked on the door downstairs, I was surprised when the door behind me opened unexpectedly. That guy with the unhealthy complexion was looking out at me.

"You want something?"

While I was explaining my errand, that same small boy peered out from beside him.

"Oh, I see. Well, thanks for your trouble."

He closed the door after speaking.

Next day, I answered a knocking at my door and found Aya-chan standing there.

"Thanks for last night. That's my older brother."

She smiled, then immediately closed the door. Having seen her face for only a moment, I didn't get a clear impression, but from the look of her eyes she seemed tired out. There was happiness in her words, though, when she said, "That's my older brother," and I thought I could sense some emotional warmth coming through.

So I had spoken with Aya-chan for the first time. It had become inevitable, since a stranger, who by rights had no reason to visit me, had chanced to stop by. This was a common, trivial matter, of course, but it was risky. It wouldn't have meant a great deal if we'd only spoken out of necessity, but there was that warmth I felt. Having gone downstairs with the message for her, I now also clearly understood her relationship to the tattooist, Horimayu-san: she was his lover. It might have been just the slightest encounter, but my sensing the warmth in her heart couldn't help but come to his attention sooner or later.

I went to the shrine grounds. Sure enough, the chicken from the other day was now one-eyed. A chill ran through my whole body when I saw it.

One morning several days later, as I was going to the toilet, I could tell that someone was already in the apartment across the hall; I could hear the voice of somebody in pain. Apparently the tattooist had been at work since before I woke up that day. After Sai-chan came and left, I could tell that he stopped by there, too.

That afternoon, the door across the hall was standing half open when I came back from picking up lunch at the Sanwa Market. In the cramped four-and-a-half-mat room, barely nine feet square, I could see a naked man lying facedown and Horimayu-san jabbing his back with a needle. I wanted to see more, but I couldn't very well stand there looking. All I saw, for just a moment, were a man's naked thighs and buttocks and Horimayu-san's wiry back. Every time I heard the man's grunts of pain I vividly imagined Horimayu-san holding his breath, thrusting in the needle.

To see—to witness accidentally, rather—is a fearsome thing. Until then, I had only overheard the sounds of suffering. Now I had accidentally witnessed the scene in that legend about the crane who married the poor peasant, bloodying herself as she plucked out her own feathers one by one to make the warp and weft for weaving on the loom. While processing beef and pork organs in my apartment, I mentally compared my work to what I sensed about the activity in the room across the hall. My hands, too, were slimy with organ blood and fat. Something about that suffocating intensity, the gasps of pain as the needle struck each time, couldn't help but eat into my heart and soul. It was the breath of agony and the bloodshot eyes that accompanied the stabbing of the needle into human skin—no, into the living human spirit. Why would anyone let ink be rubbed into his flesh at the expense of such grotesque suffering? What was the lure of such luminosity that anyone would endure being driven half mad to have it carved into his body?

"Oh, hello, Seiko Nēsan!"

I could hear Aya-chan's voice out in the hall. She had come out of the room across the way just as Seiko Nēsan was about to enter my apartment. The little boy was clinging to Aya-chan's legs, saying, "Shit! Shit! Shit!"

"Just look at his face, Seiko Nēsan. Shimpei's been stung by a bee."

"Oh, you poor thing. And such a handsome face, too."

"He said he hit a bees' nest with a stick on the way home from school—whoa, what do you think you're doing?"

After this exchange, Seiko Nēsan came in with the boy in tow; meanwhile, Aya-chan went somewhere nearby to buy medicine. His face was swollen around the eyes and on the upper lip. He kept grimacing; no doubt it hurt pretty badly. Taking a sweet bean-paste dumpling wrapped in an oak leaf out of her bag, Seiko Nēsan joked, "With a face like that, Shimpei-chan, I don't guess you could eat this even if I gave it to you."

"I don't like 'em anyway!" His answer was defiant, but on the heels of these words he began to tell his story with some pride, evidently seeking her sympathy: "Naitō-kun kept saying yesterday, 'I found a bees' nest, I found a bees' nest,' so I went and found it today, because he wouldn't say where it was, and so I found it, and then Sumiko-chan says, 'I don't like bees, Shimpei-chan, how about you?' So I told her I'd knock it down for her, and then I had to hit it, but she just hollered and then she said she was gonna tell, she was gonna tell Miss Fujie."

"Oh, so now I see. I'll bet you like that little girl, what's-her-name, Sumiko-chan, don't you?

"No way. She kept saying she was gonna tell, she was gonna tell Miss Fujie on me."

"This Miss Fujie—isn't she that good-looking schoolteacher that comes into my place for a drink now and then?"

No answer.

"Shimpei-chan, you poor guy, the little gal's double-crossed you. That Sumiko-chan sounds like a bad number to me."

"Oh, no, she makes me origami things all the time, even."

"Oh-ho! So that's why you knocked the bees' nest down. How cute! You silly thing."

Just then, Aya-chan came back from the pharmacy. As she put salve on his face and applied cold compresses to the inflammation, they rehashed the story of Sumiko-chan and everybody broke out laughing. No doubt in his own way the little boy had been dead serious when he went to knock down the bees' nest. But all he got for his trouble was a little girl's cruel words, and he came home with his face all swollen. In his innocence, though, he stuck up for the little girl when Seiko Nēsan criticized her and thus invited another round of laughter. I couldn't help thinking just then about his father, squatting alone in the courtyard of the shrine. That afternoon was the first time since I arrived that there'd been even a brief moment of warmth in that apartment.

Seiko Nēsan stood up and said, "Well, I guess it's time for me to go," and on that note the three of them left. Afterward, only Aya-chan's scent remained in the room. I opened the window. Right outside, however, was the wall of the house next door. I opened the hall door, too, but her scent took a long time to fade. I ate the leaf-wrapped sweet dumpling Seiko Nēsan had brought. The sweets she brought were always high-quality traditional Japanese confections. I knew from this that she was being thoughtful, but I hadn't forgotten her grasping my hand the first time I entered the apartment.

As always at night, the usual feeling of solitude came over me. There was neither a television set nor a telephone in this apartment. I never got any letters, of course. Other than the people I was dealing with here, the only person who knew I was here was Kanida, the one who provided me with the introduction. I didn't know a thing about Kanida, however: he was just another customer of unknown background who used to come into that cheap bar in Nishinomiya. He was a baby-faced man with shifty eyes, and I fell for his line of goods. When I got here, however, I was amazed to learn that Kanida knew things about me. I hadn't told anybody since abandoning my life in Tokyo about having a college education, yet things like that have a way of getting around without your knowing about it. Kanida was probably somehow tied in with these people here. I had no real idea, of course, what sort of place "here" really was.

As I lay thinking in the darkness, the stench of spoiled meat juices assailed my nostrils. It was gradually becoming hotter; the putrid odor was growing stronger and stronger with every day of summer's approach. Summer is the season of decay. Aya-chan's scent still lingered, ever so faintly, in the midst of that stench. In the darkness downstairs, she might have been locked in Horimayu-san's embrace: Horimayu-san, who tenaciously jabbed needles into human bodies, always with those bloodshot eyes, as though possessed. Maybe a man like him, who made his living single-mindedly stabbing tattoos into living souls, had no other means of working off his sins.

The substance of love can take many forms. When I first started work at the *okonomiyaki* restaurant in Kobe, the good-looking owner of the place told me, "You know, Ikushima-san, they say, 'scratch my back, and I'll scratch yours.' You do your best at your job, and one day I'll give you a massage right here." As she said that, she slipped her hand between my knees where I was sitting on the tatami-mat floor.

That night I wasn't yet hearing any voices from next door, but I imagined that before long some godforsaken woman, tormented by feelings of damnation, would be dragging in some equally lonely lost soul. They would copulate as though starved for sex, seeking some solace in their lives; then would come that bizarre chanting in an unintelligible tongue.

But why had I come here? Why had I fallen so easily for Kanida's whispered blandishments? Of course, I was ready to go for broke to make a living at the time: there was that, but it was the currents of some other force that had carried me here. While working in that cheap bar in Nishinomiya, I kept wishing I wasn't there. I had the same thoughts in Kobe, in Kyoto before that, and in Himeji even before that. No, the force that pushed me along from place to place had already emerged while I was in Tokyo, before all of that. I was living with a certain kind of fear, a fear of burying my life day after day in advertising sales. I felt a bitterness inside that could not be healed. I clung to my own incompetence, not even capable of becoming dependent on some woman. I was a difficult, despicable man. Without question, that had brought me to a dead end in Tokyo. Was I now going to feel that I didn't want to be here in Amagasaki either?

6

"Mister, what's "man with a past" mean?"

Shimpei came into my apartment. Having come in here once the day before, the boy had now made himself at home.

"A past?"

"Yeah. Pop and Aya-chan were talking about you and said, "He's a man with a past.""

No one was in the apartment across the hall today; that's probably why he came upstairs. He never came up when Horimayu-san was at work across the hall. I suppose the boy had been told not to, or he just might not have wanted to see anyway. I decided to act unconcerned.

"Your name's Ikushima Yoichi, right, Mister?"

I was startled. He must have sensed that I would be easy to handle. I returned his look calmly, but he showed no sign of flinching, even though his face still had the wet compresses on it to suppress the inflammation.

"Come on, Mister, wanna play cards?"

I was startled to see Shimpei pull a pack of cards out of his pocket.

"It's fun. Some people get dealt a great hand and still go bust."

Here he was, at his tender age, already a gambling shark.

"Listen, Shimpei, I've got work to do. Let's play some other time."

He gave up surprisingly easily and left. After watching him go, I was left with a lingering feeling that I had done something cruel. Besides that, I felt a little blindsided to have learned that Horimayu-san and Aya-chan had been talking about me. "Man with a past" had a somehow ludicrous ring to it. They probably picked up the line from some movie, but what had they read into my past? There had been no real incidents to speak of, not even so much as getting fired for embezzling company money. If there'd been anything to talk about at all, it might have been the time a certain woman looked at me out of the corner of her eye, said, "Well, that's it," then turned her back and walked away toward the concourse of Yotsuya Station. It was a night in April and it had snowed, unusual for Tokyo. As I watched her walk off, I thought, *she's running away.* I wanted her to stop, turn around, and look at me one more time, but she went quickly out of sight. This sort of thing happens to people all the time, of course; it's an everyday matter. Maybe the only not-everyday thing was the snow in Tokyo in April. I wondered what had escaped from within me.

This sort of thing was peanuts, though, compared to what Seiko Nēsan had shared with me. My life had no "content"; hers did. She was harboring the most unspeakable part of her life in her soul, living every day with the raw wound. What made her confession so terrifying to me was the realization that I had nothing similar to reveal.

Of course she had confided in me, no doubt because I was an outsider. This was one basket case she had surely misread, but that was fine with me. I wondered, though, if her mind had

somehow reached a state of emptiness now that she had con-
fessed to me. Had she attained release, now that she'd confided
the most difficult part of her life to this empty human being
named Ikushima? So far, I hadn't given her a single thing in
return. I had nothing to offer. Even had I wanted to recipro-
cate, to tell her of some part of my life too difficult to reveal, I
couldn't have come up with anything of the sort. Being so curt
with Shimpei was probably not unconnected with this.

Already quite a few strangers had intruded rudely into my
mind since I arrived here in Ama. If I counted among these
alien intruders all the men who had passed through Seiko
Nēsan's body, the number of such strangers would be legion.
But clearly I was still afraid of reaching out to these people of
my own will, especially afraid of touching them directly. So far
I had responded with nothing but silence, but was there really
any other way?

One night, there was loud shouting from the apartment next
door. "What the hell's the matter with you—? Oh, my God!
Throwing up! Look what you did!" It was the sound of a woman's voice, almost a scream. There was a flurry of footsteps.
After pounding on my door, a fiftyish woman pushed her way
in. I had never seen her before. She had nothing on but a slip.

"Hey, you got any—any medicine? That asshole's spit up
blood." She suddenly looked panicked, blurted out, "Oh!" and
ran back to the next apartment.

Following her, I looked in and saw her hastily putting on a
skirt next to a naked man who was lying facedown in obvious
pain.

"Don't look!"

Abruptly she shoved me back into the corridor and followed
me out. After fumbling with the key to lock the door, she ran

down the stairs breathlessly. I could hear groans coming from behind the door. He was nearly bald. I retreated to my own place, turned out the light, and kept quiet. Shortly afterward, I heard the pounding of several people's footsteps going into the apartment next door. "Okay, you get his legs. Oh shit, he's already— What do we do with his shorts? Take 'em with you, dumb-ass." It was a mixture of male and female voices. I could hear them carrying the stricken man downstairs in another flurry of footsteps. They probably were not taking him to a hospital.

But then, somebody came back upstairs. Just one. The footsteps stopped outside my apartment. I picked up a short, sharp-pointed knife. The lock on my door was broken. The door opened slightly.

"Sorry we bothered you, sir." He had an intimidating voice. I heard his footsteps again as he went down the stairs.

Seiko Nēsan came by the next day. Wordlessly smoking her cigarette as usual, she watched me out of the corner of her eye as I worked. I noticed after a little while, however, that she was singing in a low voice with a blank look in her eyes, as though in a trance.

I'm a spinning wheel, I spin the lotus threads.
Come dragons, mayflies, spiders, centipedes;
I'm the needle's point, I carry the thread of fate.
Oh, great Buddha in Nara:
I want to meet the one who suckled you at her breast.

Bent over my work, I listened intently as I cut up the meat. Her hoarse voice struck me to the heart.

"It's a nice song."

"Oh. Really?" Abruptly she stopped singing. There was a

sudden, awkward silence. I had only spoken my mind honestly, but she must have thought I was teasing. On her way out, she said, "I heard there was quite a commotion here last night." When I raised my head in surprise, she went on: "Don't worry. I've talked to that guy."

By "that guy" she must have meant the one whose voice I had heard in the dark last night. I wondered where they'd taken the bald one. If he was spitting up blood, he must have had tuberculosis. They probably dumped him somewhere, though. Men and women of that kind thought nothing of abandoning a sick person in the course of their business. The fact that Seiko Nēsan had talked to them, however, must have meant that I was now under her protection.

Over and over, I repeated to myself the words I'd heard Seiko Nēsan singing. Something about her song made it irresistible. I was reminded of another song, the kind little girls sing while bouncing a ball, one the woman who had left me at Yotsuya Station told me she learned as a child from an aunt who later committed suicide. It was long and full of nonsense syllables; it started out:

> On-kyō-Kyōbashi, nan-nan-Nakabashi,
> Tomorrow you'll be sweet sixteen;
> Put on your best kimono, with the long sleeves;
> Put on your makeup, but just a little touch:
> People will notice if you lay it on too much . . .

I could never forget that song; she had taught it to me painstakingly, practically word by word. The aunt, her father's younger sister, had raised her. "She took poison one afternoon, during an eclipse," she had said. I asked her when that was and realized that I, too, had vivid memories of the same eclipse. It was one summer while I was still a boy; I stood in a rice field in the middle of Banshū Plain on the way home from school, watching through the stiff dark plastic sheet I was holding above me. I had no way of knowing, of course, that a broken-hearted, middle-aged single woman in the Tokyo suburbs had just taken poison to end her life.

Sai-chan came by in the evening to pick up the meat. Ever since the last incident, I felt a certain strange tension whenever he came. For his part, Sai-chan betrayed no change; he acted as if nothing at all had happened. This day, though, something unexpected took place. As I was getting the meat out of the refrigerator he said, "Here, have one on me," and with a thud he set down a dark, round bottle of some foreign liquor on the tatami floor behind me.

Startled, I said, "Uh, thanks—" I couldn't think of anything else to say.

It was a late April afternoon. There was no sign of people around. A fly was circling noiselessly inside the room. There was company in the apartment across the hall. After a while, somebody left; it seemed like Horimayu-san. A short while later, Aya-chan came upstairs and went in. Considerable time passed, and then I heard: "What the hell was that? Say it again!" It was Aya-chan's shrill voice. "All right, then, you take this shit and get the hell out. Don't think you can put one over on me, just because I'm a woman. You want a fight? I'll take you on any time."

I thought I heard scuffling, and then there was a thud.

"Hey, hey, take it easy, Aya-chan, I was just k-kidding, OK?"

"Take your filthy money and get out!"

When I stepped out into the corridor with the bloody knife in my hand, I saw a man, fiftyish, whom I took to be some kind of small-time merchant. Seeing me, he looked shocked and then turned around to call out over his shoulder to Aya-chan, "You're going to regret this, you—you—!"

He scurried out as he spoke, dragging a shoe that had come halfway off. Aya-chan shot me a sharp look and slammed the door. Just then I saw Shimpei, the little boy, standing at the end of the hallway. I, too, closed my door.

7

It was one afternoon during a long holiday weekend in May. The old married pair who lived downstairs were picking through the dump near the apartment building, looking for things they could use or food still fit to eat. I had often seen such sights while living in Tokyo and Kobe, but here they didn't seem like just an old couple picking through garbage. Instead, the forlorn backs of this old pair quietly living out their lives downstairs appeared to me the image of devout spirits. The sky was so blue it stung my eyes.

I looked around and realized that flowers were blossoming, even in the middle of this town. Weeds were springing up along the roads; azaleas flamed; white Japanese roses bloomed behind a fence. As I walked, I picked an azalea blossom and sucked the nectar. The shadowy forms of out-of-work drifters loitered in front of the train station.

When I came home, I found at my door a tract from some off-brand religious sect. After some rather farfetched expositions of doctrine came a passage that impressed me:

Just once, try jumping into the fire; then you will truly realize how hot it is. Being a clever person, you may think you don't need to do such a thing to know that it's hot, but only those who have been through the fire are qualified to say, "it's hot." The words you utter then will be the words of God. They are the words of Life. Someone who has not been through the fire who says "it's hot" is only speaking empty words, mere words that do not partake of Life. You, yourself, know this better than anyone else. In the beginning, when words were with God alone, they conveyed the Truth. Only when words became the property of Man did they begin to transmit falsehood. Inconveniently enough, however, words in Man's ownership also occasionally happen to convey the truth. To answer the question: the truth is nothing other than what is blessed by God, but humans have no idea of what is truly pleasing to God's will. Hence, Man smugly lies. What drives him to lie is nothing but the conceit within him; it is significant that the Chinese character for the word "lie" consists of two parts that can be read separately as "the work of man." Nevertheless, the fact that Man's words occasionally do convey the truth is due to the presence of something within him that is beyond his understanding—*mono*. This is the *mono* in many Japanese words that refers to primitive matters of the mind and spirit, the *mono* that sometimes destroys men. However . . .

The Sunday morning following the end of the long weekend, I couldn't stand to stay in the apartment, so I went outside. In the Deyashiki district, I caught sight of a small white butterfly fluttering around in the street. Surprised, I followed it, but it soon disappeared. On the spur of the moment I decided I wanted to go to Nara, thinking that I might see some butterflies if I wandered around a field somewhere in the Nara Basin. I had not been to Nara since a school trip during sixth grade.

As the train began to run along the Yamato River, the fresh green of the fields and hills stung my eyes. Impulsively I got off the train at Hōryūji Station. I didn't go toward the famous temple there, however; instead, I walked along the narrow dirt paths that ran crisscross between the rice paddies. It was before rice-planting season in the fields; milk-vetch bloomed along the paths, and larks were singing. No one was out doing farm work this time of year, since they no longer grew wheat hereabouts. Yellow rapeseed was blooming in the distance, and I could see the farmhouses' white plastered walls. Above them swam bright-colored cloth carp streamers celebrating Boy's Day, and farther beyond appeared the roofs of Buddhist temples. There are people who make a living taking photographs of scenes like this; that's why I felt uncomfortable seeing this scenery actually in front of me, as if its significance had somehow been defiled. I walked and walked but saw no butterflies.

I got a little tired and sat down by the road among the rice fields. I watched the beautifully clear sky while eating the rice balls I had bought at Osaka Station. This sky at least surely hadn't changed since Prince Shōtoku, weary from his struggles against the powerful nobles, gazed up at it nearly fourteen hundred years ago. Thinking that I was in a similar state made me feel rather melancholy. I, too, would eventually vanish from the earth. Realizing that quite a bit of time had gone by, I got up and strolled back along the path through the rice fields, making noises with a whistle I had crafted from a weed stem.

Suddenly, I was startled by a snake that raced across the path right in front of me. For some reason, ever since childhood I have clearly remembered every encounter with a snake. It's puzzling; I remember those incidents very vividly, as if they were imbued with some special glow.

I walked along the road lined with pine trees that led toward Hōryūji Temple. In front of the main gate stood an emaciated beggar with a red-haired dog in tow. The dog was drooling and covered with mange.

Several days later, Shimpei came to visit me again. "Would you fold me a paper airplane, Mister?"

He had been playing alone in the vacant lot behind the apartment building and glanced up at me when I came back from picking up something for lunch. That's when I recalled how he looked standing at the end of the corridor several days before; he probably wanted to approach me, but to accept him into my company was to take yet another step into the world that lurked in the background behind him. Nevertheless, I could no longer refuse.

"Look, Shimpei-chan, my hands are dirty. I can't make you a paper airplane right now."

"How about telling me a story, then?"

"A story, huh? Well . . . "

"Mister, have you ever been left in a forest?"

"What?"

"You see, Miss Fujie read us the story of Hansel and Gretel in school today. They got left in the forest. Mister, why did they have to have a stepmother?"

I felt a shock.

"Snow White gets left in a forest because of a stepmother, too, doesn't she? I asked Miss Fujie why, but she just shook her head and said, 'Yes, why would that be?'"

I tried to visualize his mother. I couldn't make out her facial features, but she appeared as a dim dark shape. When "Hansel and Gretel" and "Snow White" were read to this child, he had recognized the theme beneath the stories' surface, of children rejected by their mother.

"Hansel and Gretel's stepmother and Snow White's step-mother left their children in the forest because they were both bad people, Shimpei-chan. That's all. You have Aya-chan, don't you?"

"Yeah, but she's not my mom."

"I see . . . so she's your big sister."

"No, that woman's not my big sister."

I was stung by the phrase "that woman." The words seemed totally out of place coming from a child.

"Then what is she?"

Suddenly I was seized with the urge to ask a cruel question. In his own way, this child was sharing with me the deepest part of his own existence. I remembered Horimayu-san as he squatted alone in the shrine courtyard. Was Shimpei's mother divorced or separated from Horimayu-san, or was she dead? In any case, he must feel somehow as if he, too, had been aban-doned in the forest. I decided to cut to the chase and ask him point-blank what he knew.

"So what happened to your mom?"

"You know, Miss Fujie's going to get married pretty soon. She told us that today while she read us the story of the Princess in the Ashes. You know, Cinderella."

This was one sharp kid. And what a brilliant flash of feminine nature, too, for Miss Fujie to tell her own Cinderella story after reading the Grimm brothers' harsh stories to these children. "Cinderella" is also a tale about a stepchild's sufferings. Shim-pei must have had that fully in mind as he dodged my question.

Ever since Aya-chan tongue-lashed the small-time merchant type, Horimayu-san had stopped coming up to the apartment across the hall. I saw no sign of Aya-chan, either. After that night, the women also quit bringing their johns to the room next door. Seiko Nēsan quit coming, too.

The only visitor I had was Sai-chan on his twice-a-day visits. I still hadn't opened the liquor bottle he had left. I kept it on top of the refrigerator, so he was sure to notice it when he came. There was no telling what kind of confrontation I might get caught up in if I continued to leave it unopened, but I was somehow hesitant to just casually open it and finish it off. And yet I had not a bit of interest in hiding the bottle from Sai-chan; open or not, I wanted to leave it out where he could see it. It seemed like the right thing to do, out of regard for him. Besides, it wasn't out of the question to think that it might end up with the two of us drinking together in my apartment. Secretly I looked forward to that, but all he did was glance at the bottle each time he came.

One day I noticed a white *dokudami* flower blooming in the alley by the apartment building. It brought back special memories for me. When I grabbed its stem and ripped it up by its roots, its distinctive, stifling smell assailed my nostrils. I went back to my apartment, opened the bottle Sai-chan had left, and took a deep swig. I poured the rest of it gurgling down the sink. I filled the empty bottle with water, stuck the single *dokudami* blossom into it, and set it back on top of the refrigerator. Sai-chan came by that evening, but as usual all he did was give the bottle a brief glance.

Seiko Nēsan came by for the first time in several days. Naturally, the first thing she saw was the white flower on top of the refrigerator.

"Well, look what you did!" she said.

That was unexpected. It was a cry of surprise, for sure, but one never knew what this woman was thinking. I had thought she probably wouldn't say anything about the flower, even if she did notice it, but for a moment she actually sounded impressed.

Ever since I had heard her singing that song, I had been planning to ask her about it the next time she came to visit. "Uh, don't get me wrong; I'm not kidding you—I can't get that song off my mind since I heard you singing it the other day."

"Really?"

"It's a nice song. I copied it into my notebook."

"You do some weird things."

"Pardon me?"

"Don't you think I'm right? This flower here's another case. A grown man like you, acting like some moonstruck girl."

I was speechless.

"Just like Shimpei's paper folding."

"I see . . . "

"It still hasn't sunk into your thick head. It sticks in my craw. What were you thinking, anyway, letting a guy like Kanida talk you into coming to a place like this?" There was growing irritation in her voice. "Chopping up pig and cow guts here, day in and day out. Does that really satisfy you? Don't you have better things to do?"

"Well, I don't want to sound like I'm crossing you, but I really thought your song was nice. I really wanted you to know I felt that way."

"Oh? I see. If that's all, I already heard you say that the other day." She looked bored. "Listen. I'm an ex-hooker. Don't play games with me."

No, no. I'm not playing games with you. The words almost got past my lips.

"If that's all, then why didn't you just keep your mouth shut? You said so once, so let's drop it."

"Uh—"

"It's OK with me if you drop it. Listen: I came here today because I need you to do me a favor. It's twelve thirty in the afternoon now, right? I'll bet you're going out for lunch pretty soon. Well, about ten to one—you know the phone booth in front of Deyashiki Station? There's some phone books in there, right?"

"Yes, ma'am."

"All right. Inside the book on the bottom, there's five ten-thousand-yen notes. At one on the dot, I want you to go in that phone booth and get the money without letting anybody see you."

"You say don't let anybody see me, but the ticket gate's right there in front—"

"That's why I'm asking you."

I said nothing.

"You chicken?"

"I'll do it."

I started to leave the apartment right then, but Seiko Nēsan grabbed the hem of my jacket.

"Dumb-ass! You stay here till ten to one, then go. Hurry, but keep your cool."

From things I had heard said while living in Kobe, I was sure this was the pickup for a drug deal. After she spoke, I sat staring silently at the weave pattern in the faded tatami mats until ten minutes to one. Seiko Nēsan also said nothing, which wasn't all that unusual for her, though there was something different about her grim expression as she silently bit her lip. When the time finally came and I went downstairs, I unexpectedly saw

Sai-chan and a middle-aged man I didn't recognize standing in the alley beside the apartment building. Seeing them, I couldn't help blurting out, "Oh, hi—," It irritated me to hear myself say it. Sai-chan nodded, as if acknowledging my greeting, but the other man just stood there with one hand stuck rather unnaturally into his pants pocket.

I went out into the main street. It was the same, familiar lifeless scene, but there was a tension in the air completely unlike anything I'd felt before. I walked toward the station. The late May sunshine seemed frighteningly bright. I wondered if it was fear of the police or of members of some other gang that was making Sai-chan and his partner nervous. The one thing I was determined to do when I got to the phone booth was to avoid any pretense, like acting as if I were going to actually make a call. I didn't care what happened after that.

When I got to the station, however, I ran into something totally unexpected. There was somebody in the phone booth, a workman-looking individual in a baseball cap. It made perfect sense, actually, but obviously the possibility had escaped my mind. I wondered whether I should stand and wait in front of the booth. If I stood around, I would be exposing myself that much more to whomever might be somewhere watching. Yet it would be even more stupid to look around trying to see if I could spot them.

I stood in front of the phone booth. The man inside glanced at me and turned his back. There was a stack of three phone books at the level of his knees. I looked at the station clock; it was two minutes to one already, so according to Seiko Nēsan the money should already be hidden in the phone book. The clock moved past 1:02. I was starting to get edgy. It was a long call. It had been only about four minutes, but I could sense in every pore of my body the eyes that were no doubt observing me intently from some unseen hiding place.

I was staring a hole in the man's back. The tension was suffocating. The afternoon sun of May felt even more fearfully bright. It's a fact of life that we don't know what will happen at any given time and place. The scene would have appeared perfectly mundane to anyone unaware of the facts, just a man waiting his turn outside a telephone booth, but the view in front of me was strangely, blindingly bright. On the clock, 1:09 went by. I was startled when the man suddenly came out of the booth; I could see his face clearly.

I went into the booth and hastily pulled out the phone book from the bottom of the stack. The two that were on top fell unexpectedly at my feet, and I felt a chill go up my spine. Just then, somebody came and stopped outside the booth. It was a young man. The chill shot through me from the top of my head to the soles of my feet. He had a face that looked as if it had been crushed inward from both sides. My fingers slipped wildly as I turned the pages. The ten-thousand-yen notes suddenly came into sight. Snatching them up, I simultaneously turned around and pushed the phone booth door outward. I could see the young man's face very clearly. The door wouldn't open: I was pushing in the wrong place. My pulse was pounding.

When I finally got out, the air around me seemed even brighter and felt as if it were swirling around me. My throat was parched. Feeling as though I were being followed, I started walking fast. Suddenly it occurred to me that I still had the ten-thousand-yen notes crumpled up in my fist; I hurriedly stuffed them into my pocket, and then realized with a start that I hadn't counted them. I stuck my hand back into my pocket, counting the notes as I walked faster. At that moment, I was reminded of the man I had seen in the alley next to the apartment house as I was leaving; at the thought of his hand, I felt a disgust that was intense enough to make me grit my teeth. My foot slipped. I turned around, gripped by an indefinable sense of panic. All I saw was the same familiar scene in front of the train station, but it was also not the same familiar scene. A man was walking behind me. He didn't seem to be following me, but I couldn't help picking up my pace. I couldn't tell for sure at that speed if I actually had five notes in my pocket. No longer able to stand it, I pulled out the money and counted it. There were five notes. *Is this all it's about?* I thought. It began to feel as though I had been making a fool of myself. I jammed the money back into my pocket.

When I got back to the alley by the apartment house, Sai-chan and his companion were no longer there. Now that I was in the shade, I could tell that I was soaked all over in sweat; it stuck to me like an uncomfortable feeling of humiliation. Seiko Nēsan was waiting for me in the apartment, sitting formally on the tatami floor with her knees together. Raising herself up a little, she said, "Oh, thank goodness it's you," and looked at my face. Then she let her legs take a more relaxed position and seemed to let out a sigh of relief. Evidently she had been waiting there in that uncomfortable posture the whole time I was gone at the station plaza. I breathed heavily as I took the money out of my pocket.

"Sorry to put you through all that."

"Oh, no, I didn't mind."

"Over a piddling amount of money, too. After you went, I thought maybe I should have gone, after all . . . "

"No, really . . . "

At that moment, it occurred to me that Seiko Nēsan's once- or twice-a-week visits might have been due to her regularly taking care of this business by herself. It seemed likely. In any case, I felt something almost like gratitude at the thought of her sitting there stiffly the whole time, waiting for me, while I went to the phone booth and back.

Sai-chan came by the next morning as usual with his load of beef and pork organs and poultry. It was remarkable that this man could always behave as though absolutely nothing had happened the day before. I was dissatisfied with that, though, and I spoke to him as though taking careful aim.

"Sai-chan."

He looked startled.

"Thanks for that liquor the other day."

"What, that stuff? No big deal."

"How about us going for a drink someplace around here one day?"

"No, thanks."

He walked out, as if shrugging off my words.

8

The woman who ran the sundries shop downstairs had eyes like a sleepy cat. When I went in to buy dishwashing liquid right after I arrived, I saw her swallow a raw egg. I never went back in there.

I went to Sanwa Market to buy soap, razor blades, and such. Even a recluse needs things like that. Just as I was about to leave the market, I caught sight of Aya-chan standing under the eaves, opening her umbrella. It had been several days since I last saw her. She turned in the opposite direction from the apartment house and walked off down the shabby back street toward Hanshin Amagasaki Station. I watched her go, then opened my own umbrella and started walking without taking my eyes off her back. After going a little way, I began to feel my heart pounding. It must have been from the excitement of knowing I was tailing her. Aya-chan's umbrella had a bright red-flower pattern, and I could see the black hair falling over her shoulders. After going about a block, she turned to the left. I felt the urge to start running but suppressed it and kept on walking. I looked to the left when I got to the corner where she had turned, but she had disappeared.

I went on to the main shopping district in town, then returned home after buying a box of twelve colored crayons and a sketch-book at a stationery store. As always, the woman in the sundries shop downstairs looked at my shopping bag with her sleepy-cat eyes. The sudden disquieting feeling that came over me after I unthinkingly started following Aya-chan, and the emptiness I felt when she vanished: these seemed like the signs that appear when *words* begin to take shape inside a human being. I wondered, too, if the time weren't approaching for me to leave this town. With such baseless thoughts rolling around in my head, I went back to butchering organs in my apartment. Outside the window was the steady sound of rain.

Seiko Nēsan came by.

"We've sure been getting a lot of rain every day," she said. I swallowed an expression of surprise; she had never been so chatty before when she came. "Rainy days get me down."

This reminded me of a line from a poem by Nakano Shige-haru: *Rain is something like love.*

At my age I was still ignorant of things like love, kindness, and other such emotions contained in *words*; yet my mind was stuffed with strangers' words like these.

"You told me the other day that you liked my singing, didn't you?"

"Yes, sorry about that."

"Oh, no, that's fine."

At that point, I sensed that she had just a touch of alcohol on her breath.

"You ran that little errand for me and didn't act like you minded a bit."

"That wasn't any problem—"

"One false move, and they'd have ganged up and beat the shit out of you, you know."

"Oh."

"Over peanuts. You really saved me."

"I see. I'm really a coward, so I was pretty scared."

"But everybody's that way, honey. That's why I asked you to do it. I'm sorry as hell I did."

"No, don't—"

"I really didn't want to use you like that . . . you mind if I sing again right now? "

That was a surprise.

"Hate to bother you while you're working."

"Oh, no, I—"

I was sure Seiko Nēsan had come here because she had grown restless after drinking all afternoon and listening to the ceaseless rain. Of course, everybody oozes oil out their ass like that; that's life.

> "O-gin's ninety-nine, getting wed in Kumano;
> Lost her back teeth before the wedding day,
> She's still got her front teeth, safe to say,
> Dyed those front teeth black as night,
> Pins in her hairs, just three, so white.
> She put on her bright red clothes . . . diddle-dum . . .

"That's a song from Iga Province, where I was born."

"It's kind of funny."

"Yeah—who knows, I might end up marrying like old O-gin, at ninety-nine."

I laughed, but I resolutely kept on working. Seiko Nēsan might have been drunk, but she was no pushover.

"Whatcha looking like that for?

Old father Saigyō, you waded the dry creek,
Stubbed your toe on a jellyfish bone;
Burned your throat on a tofu stick,
What'll you put on it to make it well?
Pick a mushroom from the sea,
Gather some seaweed off a hill;
Dig some clams from a mountain patch,
Roast some snow from a summer storm;
Put that on, and you'll be all right . . . "

Both those songs had hidden, randy meanings. They were quite a bit different in flavor from the lotus-thread song I had heard the other day. The words might have been whimsical, but there was no mistaking the sadness in Seiko Nēsan's heart as she sang in her raspy voice. I had no doubt she was singing these risqué songs with a throat already corroded by unspeakably painful emotions. There was no way I could offer a platitude like "nice song." When she left, immediately after she finished singing, there was a forcefulness in her manner that suggested she wanted no inane compliments from me.

I went to a nearby diner to eat supper. I was the only customer. Right in front of me was a TV showing a documentary film about the history of refugee populations spawned by wars and revolutions across the face of the earth during the twentieth century. Some of these tens of millions of people with no place to live in this world were wandering in long lines through snow and desert sand. Watching the film footage in black and white, I thought to myself, *joblessness means becoming a wanderer.*

9

Things had been quiet for a while in the apartment across the hall. There had not been a single visitor, so there was also no sign of Horimayu-san. The women, however, had begun to bring their johns to the room next door again. Again I was hearing those weird incantations that sounded vaguely like Buddhist prayers or magical spells. As I listened to them in the dark, I couldn't help thinking about Seiko Nēsan singing her songs in that hoarse voice. There was the same expression of despair, of unbearable suffering from the world's woes, but I could not have made a comment like "nice mantras" to these low, rhythmic chants. Seiko Nēsan had no doubt recited such cryptic formulas to herself as some man tongued her private parts. It's a painful thing for a human being to be human. I suppose it's from enduring that sorrow, or perhaps from being unable to endure it, that *words* are born within each of us.

Aya-chan came in unexpectedly. "Here, try some of these." She had brought some cherries in a glass bowl. They still had beads of water on them where they had just been washed.

"Thank you very much."

Aya-chan sat down on the tatami with her legs tucked up

beside her and took out a cigarette. I remembered trailing her several days ago. "Here you are, doing the same damn thing day in and day out. Seiko Nēsan was talking about it, you know."

"How so?"

"She was saying, 'Is that all he wants out of life?'"

"This is fine with me."

"Really?" Aya-chan looked downward. Her eyes always seemed to sparkle, but when they were downcast her expression became noticeably clouded. She might not have recognized that expression if she looked in a mirror, however. "Why don't you take a break and have one?"

"Oh, thanks." As I picked up a cherry, I glanced at the fullness of her breasts.

"Why'd you come to a place like this, anyway?"

"You ask why, but . . . "

"I know. You can't explain it, right?"

"Well, no—"

"Seiko Nēsan said something funny about you."

"What was that?"

"She said you were like the mummy of some boy from ancient times that somehow came to life in the modern world."

I forced a wry smile.

"She said you wouldn't be able to make it in this world. Say, you sort of got your butt in a crack the other day, didn't you?"

"Uh—You knew about that?"

"Sure. I was watching you."

"What? From where?"

All she did in response was give me a knowing look. If she was telling the truth, it must have been a highly amusing show for her. "But you were risking your life doing Seiko Nēsan a favor. You really were."

"Oh, no, I—"

"But it's true. By the way, four or five days ago—you followed me, didn't you?"

I gulped. She looked at me sharply.

"I wouldn't do things like that if I were you."

I was speechless. She kept her eyes on me.

"Everybody's watching you, you know."

She stubbed out her cigarette, shot me one last glance, and left.

I was in shock. I felt as though my identity had suddenly evaporated. I couldn't get back to my work until Sai-chan came that evening. The fresh glow of the cherries remained, lingering in sight. I had done something beyond retrieval; the memory of Aya-chan walking away in the rain filled me with deep fear. Apologizing wouldn't help now. I ate the cherries after supper, but none of them had any flavor for me any more; I felt their blandness all the way to the core of my being. I wondered what would happen if Horimayu-san heard about my trailing Aya-chan.

At lunchtime the next day, I worked up the courage to go downstairs and return the glass bowl. I was surprised when a young, rough-looking stranger opened the door; I couldn't tell if Aya-chan was in the apartment or not. When I walked outside, the surroundings seemed to me even more threatening than they did that other afternoon. Wherever I looked, it felt as though someone were watching me from the shadows.

10

"Mister, did you fold that paper airplane for me?"

Shimpei came into the apartment. I had idly promised the other day that I would fold him one, but the piece of paper, some kind of wrapping material, was still there just as he'd left it. Shimpei glanced at the paper, then glanced at me, and left without saying another word.

I folded the paper airplane for him. I had bought the twelve-color set of crayons and sketchbook to make him happy, but I couldn't help thinking there was no point in it right now. As I hastily struggled to think of an excuse to offer him, I sensed a baseness in myself; in that respect, I was indisputably already a deceitful adult.

I took the crayons out of the closet and looked at the twelve colors lined up in a row. I had bought them because I remembered how delighted I had been as a boy when my aunt surprised me with a twelve-color set of crayons just like these. When I told an acquaintance about this once, he replied, "Really? You know, I've had the same experience. Odd thing about crayons, isn't it?" There's definitely something about crayons that can brighten your spirits for a moment.

I don't know how it happened, but the picture of a flowering iris I once drew during art class in grade school was sent to the White House to represent all of Japan's elementary school students in honor of General Dwight David Eisenhower's inauguration as president of the United States of America. Japan was no longer under military occupation, but at the time there was still a strong sense that Japan was a US dependency. The adults talked to each other over a copy of the newspaper with the article. It was the first time I had enjoyed the pleasure of having my name become famous, and my first case of being poisoned by fame. For a first-grader, it was something totally unexpected.

To me, more than twenty years later, living isolated in a tenement in a town like Amagasaki, all this was nothing more than a fleeting memory. To be recalling such things was probably a sign of the poison still strong in my system.

I went downstairs to find Shimpei. He wasn't in the alley, so I thought he might be in his apartment, but I couldn't bring myself to look for him there. When I went out to the vacant lot in back for a change of mood, I caught a glimpse of Shimpei's head. Construction materials were stockpiled there; kicking his heels in the air, he was peeking down into one of several terracotta drainpipes that had been stood on end. He looked around as if startled when I stopped and stood behind him.

"What are you looking at?" I asked.

"Don't look!"

I was taken aback at his unexpectedly harsh response. "Here you go." I said.

As I spoke, I launched the paper airplane that I had been holding in my hand. He gave a shout like "Wow!" and ran off after it. While he was busy with that, I looked down into the pipe. There was a large toad crouched in the bottom. Picking up the paper airplane, Shimpei shouted as he turned back toward me.

"You looked at it, didn't you?"

"At what?"

"The toad."

"What—you've got a toad in here?"

A sudden look of distress crossed Shimpei's face.

"Well, then, why don't you let me have a look?" I said.

He came running and acted as if he were trying to protect the pipe from me. The toad was as big as a man's skull.

"If you look at it, it'll die!"

"What?"

"Don't look at it!"

Shimpei shouted frantically and spread his arms wide. I didn't know how many days that toad had been imprisoned in the pipe, but it would probably die soon, now that I had seen it. Shimpei kept his arms spread, his teeth clenched.

While I was in the apartment cutting up meat, Shimpei came in.

"Mister, don't tell. Don't tell Aya-chan about it."

"About what?"

"The toad."

"I won't. I didn't see it, anyway."

Shimpei began to show signs of relief.

"Was it you that put it in the pipe?"

"Yeah. I caught it with my bare hands."

"Wow. Pretty big, isn't it?"

"Yeah, it is. Like this." He gestured with his hands to show its size.

"Well, then, would you let me see it?"

"No. If you look at it, it'll die."

"Why?"

"Because . . . because it'll die if anybody looks at it." The kid was saying he had coolly caught that huge toad with his bare hands and thrown it into the pipe. I wondered how he was feeding it.

"Shimpei-chan. See those crayons over there?"

He turned around.

"I got them for you."

Shimpei stared at the crayons and sketchbook, but made no move to pick them up.

"What's the matter?"

"I don't like drawing pictures."

I was shocked. Then I saw a vivid image of Horimayu-san, with bloodshot eyes, stabbing a tattoo into someone's skin. I cursed my own stupidity. No doubt Shimpei was also picturing the images his father created in those tattoos. The thought hadn't crossed my mind when I bought the crayons and sketchbook. All I was thinking about was the delight I'd felt when my aunt surprised me with the crayons she had bought.

That night I thought about freeing the toad in the pipe. I decided, however, that its fate was sealed now that I had seen it, and went to bed. At least I lay down with that thought, but I couldn't sleep; I couldn't stop wondering why he had said it would die if I looked at it, and why he had told me not to mention it to Aya-chan. I felt as though the strange frightfulness of *words* were scorching my soul.

I turned the light back on. With the crayons Shimpei had refused, I drew a bird. It was a hunch-shouldered blue heron, the kind I had often seen in the lily ponds on the Banshū Plain, near my old home.

The next day, I went back to the vacant lot while Shimpei was at school. I trembled inwardly, but looked at the toad. It was crouched unmoving in the bottom of the pipe, waiting to die. That night, holding my breath while again drawing blue herons, that one-eyed chicken at the Ebisu Shrine came to mind; I drew a blind heron. When I looked at my finished drawing, I saw an intense vitality in it.

11

Most likely it was because Sai-chan had fumbled a job and had to be bailed out that Seiko Nēsan had sent me on that errand to the telephone booth. I didn't want to know the exact details of the situation. I did feel like having a drink with him sometime but, as always, Sai-chan never betrayed a hint that anything had happened. I wrote him off as a loser.

I saw Horimayu-san for the first time in a while. I dropped into the local diner for a late lunch and found him there silently drinking saké and snacking on pickled clams. I was suddenly reminded of having recently trailed Aya-chan. Our eyes met, and I made a slight sign of recognition, but he seemed bothered by my greeting gesture. It made me nervous. I wondered what would happen if this man found out what went on that day. Aya-chan would probably not say anything, but there was no guarantee he wouldn't hear about it if somebody else had been watching. Around here—no, anywhere she went—Aya-chan was the type who attracted constant notice. My meal had no flavor.

After I went back to my place and was at work cutting up meat, Shimpei came to visit.

"Mister, what happened to those crayons?"

"Oh, those? You said you didn't want them, so I used them to draw pictures. See? Over there."

"Hey! It's Aya-chan!"

"What?"

"Aya-chan's back's got a bird on it, too."

I gathered from what Shimpei was saying that Aya-chan had some sort of bird tattooed on her back. I imagined a fantastic tattoo adorning pale feminine flesh; at the same time, I remembered that uneasy lunch. Shimpei was also looking at the other of the two pictures, the one of the blind blue heron.

"Mister, can I take this picture to show Aya-chan?"

"No."

I had a mental image of Aya-chan's back as she walked away in the rain.

"Why not? I just want to show her."

"No. I'll give you these crayons instead, though."

"I don't like to draw pictures."

I said nothing.

"But I like stories."

I stayed silent, and after a little while, Shimpei left. I put the crayons and pictures away in the closet. Aya-chan's pale nakedness had endured tattooing and a pain that could draw forth cries like those of some demonic spirit. A kind of shadowy darkness came over Aya-chan's expression whenever her eyes were downcast; I suppose this expression was the true face of her hidden inner demon. As I was working and rolling such thoughts around in my head, Shimpei came back in looking distressed.

"You looked at my toad, didn't you, Mister?"

"What?"

"The toad's dead!"

I was speechless.

"You looked at my toad, didn't you?"

"Yes, I did."

"Shit!" As he shouted, he abruptly hurled a stone at my face.

I was startled; no sooner did I realize what he had done than the stone hit me beside one eye; there was a spatter of blood. It was my right eye. I heard Shimpei running off down the corridor. Blood smeared my hand where I held it up against my face.

The next afternoon, I ran into Horimayu-san and Aya-chan on the street in front of the apartment house as they were coming back together from somewhere. I had a sudden vision of Aya-chan's pale body. Seeing the thick gauze patch on my face, she said, "My god, what happened to your face?" and came closer.

"Oh, uh—I just slipped."

"Where?"

"Ah—right around here."

"Bullshit!" Horimayu-san spoke out sharply, looking at me. Startled, Aya-chan glanced back and forth at him and me. I drew up in fear; I could feel the hair standing on end all over me. He, however, walked on into the alley next to the building.

Gently touching the gauze on my face, Aya-chan said, "Tell me the truth. What happened to your face?"

"Well, no, really—"

"Who hit you?"

"I—uh—" I mumbled. "Excuse me."

I walked away toward Sanwa Market. Behind me, I could hear Aya-chan saying, "What the hell's the matter with you?"

I didn't know how much Horimayu-san knew about the situation, but I was shocked to realize that Shimpei had told him, and only him, about it. Also, there was no telling when Aya-chan might change her mind and decide to tell him about my trailing her. When I went by the vacant lot on the way back from the market, I found the drainpipe pushed over and the toad lying there dead, its white belly showing.

While I was eating my takeout supper, Seiko Nēsan came in; she was agitated. The moment she saw my face, she said, "What's this I hear about somebody hitting you?" Looking at me with glaring eyes, her face was like some demon mask.

"Uh, well, no, it wasn't anything, really."

"Let's see. They got your eye, didn't they?"

"Oh, my eye's all right."

"Well, that's good, but it shook me up when I heard you came into the pharmacy all bloody. Who did it? I'll give 'em hell. Come on, tell me: who did it?"

"No, really . . . " I couldn't lie about it any more, but at the same time I couldn't very well tell the truth.

"Tell me now, who was it? Don't be scared to say."

"No, no, it's really nothing."

"All right, then." She heaved a sigh and rubbed her lips with the tip of her middle finger. The matchbox-sized stone that Shimpei had thrown at me was sitting on top of the refrigerator. "Well, I've got a shop to run." She hurried back out.

12

On a rainy day in the middle of June, I took the Hankyū train to Kyoto for the first time since I arrived in Amagasaki. I was going to visit my acquaintance who lived in the Koyama-Hananoki-chō district. His name was Harada Miki, a fortyish man I had met while doing menial work in that restaurant in Kyoto. Aside from his practice as a pediatrician, he studied the philosophical works of Husserl and Merleau-Ponty, publishing occasional pieces of rambling cultural criticism in newspapers and magazines. Having no fixed address and thus no health system card, I couldn't go to regular hospitals. If I did, they would ask me a lot of awkward questions, so I decided to impose and see if he would give me some free treatment for my wound.

Whenever I was in Kyoto, I liked to stand on one of the bridges over the Kamo River and gaze at the Kitayama, the ink-wash gray mountain range that lay north of the city. It calmed my unsettled mind; it was a way of cleansing the spirit I had practiced while working there. Though it was raining that day and I couldn't see the mountains, it was still rather comforting to watch the river flow by for the first time in a long while. When I left Harada-san's house that February morning four months before, the river had been frozen over. I thought about how many bloodsucking words had left their mark on me since, though it had been less than half a year, and I felt fortunate to be there.

After examining my cut, Harada-san told me, "It's slightly infected, but there's nothing to worry about," and gave me a drug to fight the infection. He went on: "How about it? Have you picked yourself up a honey in Amagasaki? You can spend the night here if you like, but I don't have any time to spend with you." That was kind of him. He was fond of saying, "Work's an act of devotion"; he would tell a patient's mother, "Raising children's an act of devotion, you know." His offering me a night's lodging was most likely an act of devotion, too; for reasons like this, I felt a strong liking for this man. It didn't make any difference to me what he thought about Husserl or Merleau-Ponty, because I knew the words he spoke were formed in a different part of his makeup, but he devoted himself fanatically to Husserl and Merleau-Ponty just the same. That I couldn't understand. Coming into contact with Harada-san's unaffected good humor though, I felt a sense of release, as if I'd been allowed to breathe the outside air for the first time in several months. Definitely, the generosity in Harada-san's words was nothing like the stifling consideration I felt from Aya-chan and Seiko Nēsan.

Getting off the bus at the corner of Karasuma Street and Nijō Avenue, I walked in the rain to a shop that specialized in incense. I bought a sachet made of vermilion fabric with a design of green grasses on it. To put it in somewhat exaggerated terms—I had made a sort of resolution to do this. The thought that I needed to leave Amagasaki pretty soon had been eating at me for some time now. Escape wasn't the right word for it; I had nowhere in particular in mind to go next, but somehow I just knew that the time to wander on was approaching again. I intended to save the sachet as a gift of appreciation for Seiko Nēsan when the inevitable time arrived.

If I had had any resources to speak of, I would really rather have bought her a coral hair ornament—the pin that old O-gin put in her hair—but the sachet was all I could afford. It was completely out of character for Seiko Nēsan, and I was sure she would say, with a sneer, something like, "Here you go again, another girlish notion!" but I still wanted to do it. I thought about buying another sachet, one for Aya-chan; like Seiko Nēsan, she too had taught me something. I left the shop without buying it, though.

I thought about walking from there to visit Kakiden, the catering restaurant where I had held that menial job in the past. They had treated me well there, but one day I abruptly "got up and went." "Getting up and going" was the traditional restaurant trade way of saying "quitting." I got up and went without giving any particular reason; thinking back on it, I decided I had no business showing my face there again. That vague "with no particular reason" was a constant part of me, like some sort of weapon defining who I was. I walked back. Beginning to feel like giving up on myself, I walked toward the Kamo River and looked at Kitayama, shrouded in rain. I ate at a popular *okonomiyaki* restaurant in the Gion entertainment district and went back to Amagasaki.

The weather was fair the next day. I went by the vacant lot on my way to pick up lunch and saw the decomposed remains of the toad, hideously covered with bluebottle flies. Shimpei had been so fond of that toad, but once dead it was like this. There was no doubt in my mind that Shimpei himself had been deeply hurt, not only by the toad's death, but also by having thrown the stone at me. Yet I had no particular idea what to do about it.

As I walked back along the street toward the apartment house after lunch, I heard footsteps running after me and the rattle of a school backpack. I heard Shimpei's voice: "Mister Ikushima!" He stopped for an instant when I turned around, but immediately started running again and deliberately ran into me. He had a broad grin on his face. "Mister, tell me you won't forgive me, all right?"

"What?"

"Come on, say you won't forgive me!"

The boy had been thinking. I could see it in his eyes.

"Go on, say it."

I was at a loss for words, but I couldn't very well stay silent. I thought about it as I walked a little farther, and then told him, "All right. I won't forgive you."

"Why not?"

Again I was dumbstruck.

"Why won't you forgive me?"

"Well, it's because I saw your toad."

"I get it. You ate the cherries Aya-chan gave you, didn't you?"

I said nothing.

"You ate 'em, right?"

"I did."

"See there? Daddy was right."

"What's that?"

"He said, 'that clown sure brought the glass bowl back empty.'"

I swallowed a breath.

"He said you were a piece of work."

"What's so funny about eating a bowl of cherries?"

"You're sweet on Aya-chan, aren't you?"

The high noon sun of the June day hit me square in the eyes.

"When I brought the toad home, she squealed and got mad and made a face like this. Boy, was she mad." He pulled down the corners of his eyes with his fingertips. "Then she pulled her skirt up and jumped, like this. I didn't eat the cherries. Why would I want 'em? So then she took you the cherries that I didn't want to eat. She said she wondered if you'd eat 'em, and then Gō-chan said you probably would."

I said nothing.

The one he called Gō-chan must have been the man who came to the door when I took the bowl back. The story both made sense and didn't, but at least it seemed clear that Horimayu-san and this Gō-chan fellow had been downstairs the afternoon that Aya-chan brought the cherries to my apartment, and she had come up after having a discussion with them about it. Maybe Horimayu-san had even put her up to it.

If that were the case, it was possible he knew about my trailing Aya-chan, or maybe Gō-chan had told him about it. I recalled how I had stolen a look at Aya-chan's breasts that afternoon; unquestionably it had been a lustful glance. But what was so amusing about my bringing back the bowl? Maybe they were saying, "He's got nerve, hadn't he?" or something like that. If so, Horimayu-san somehow misread me.

But no, maybe I was reading too much into it. It was possible that only Gō-chan and Shimpei had been downstairs that afternoon when Aya-chan came up, and Horimayu-san had heard about the cherries only later; I wasn't sure he would have said

I was a "piece of work" knowing that I had stalked Aya-chan. Either way, the one certainty was that Aya-chan had come up to my place with some motive; that was something extraordinary. *She pulled her skirt up and jumped, like this* . . . Shimpei's words teased me in a bittersweet way.

The next day I went again to see the toad's festering corpse. When I recalled Horimayu-san's sharp voice saying, "Bullshit!" I couldn't bear to look at it; yet I couldn't take my eyes off it either. The bluebottles came back again and again, no matter how much I tried to brush them away. But why had Shimpei pleaded with me not to look at the toad in the bottom of the pipe? He had almost been wailing. Had he been embarrassed at the thought of its being seen? Why did he say that it would die if I looked at it? Since I came here I had observed many stark things about the people who live in the lower depths of this "town without vitality." It wasn't necessarily because I wanted to see such things; I suspected that in many cases my observing these people was unbearable to them. This toad died after I saw it and putrefied; what had it meant to Shimpei while it was alive? I had fearful thoughts about what might be coming.

When I got back to the apartment house, I heard voices in the unit across the hall. It was Horimayu-san and a woman; the voice was definitely not Aya-chan's. She seemed to be carrying on in a shrill tone. Since I couldn't very well stand there eavesdropping, I went into my apartment and left the door slightly ajar. Leaving the door ajar, of course, was no better than eavesdropping; thinking better of it, I shut the door with an audible slam. As I went over to the window where I always worked, however, I heard the latch—which was broken already, anyway—fall off again with a slight noise. It would have been the perfect excuse. That irritated me, though, and I went to shut the door again, but the latch fell off once more. Life is like that sometimes.

As I was working, I heard groans from the apartment across the hall. It was a woman's voice. *So that's what that shrill talking was about,* I thought. The carrying-on must have been a monologue about all she had endured in the past, and how she was determined now to go through with the pain, as she waited for the tattooing to begin. Once the ink penetrated the skin, it would be there until her body was turned to ashes. I was sure she was in an emotional state and couldn't hold anything back; still I shivered, imagining the cold look in Horimayu-san's bloodshot eyes as he listened to her in silence. I had a sensuous vision of Aya-chan's bare body.

The woman came every day after that. One afternoon when I came back from an errand, I saw a woman I didn't recognize, leaning on the wall at the top of the stairs smoking a cigarette. She looked to be in her thirties and had a reddish tint in her hair. She bowed to me the instant our eyes met. As she bowed, she seemed to be examining me from head to toe. I offered a polite look of acknowledgment and was about to walk on past when Horimayu-san came out of his apartment and called to her. "Hey!" Quickly he went back inside. She made a clicking sound behind her teeth and ground out the cigarette with her foot; the color in her face was not healthy. As if pushing me aside, she walked on toward Horimayu-san's workroom.

She came again the next day, however, and endured the agony while emitting cries and shrieks that made me think she might be dripping saliva. Each time she did, I imagined Aya-chan's naked flesh being jabbed with the tattoo needle and it spurred my lust.

One morning when Sai-chan came, he gave me a sealed

envelope and asked me to deliver it to the Igaya before the end of the day. Not another word was said about it, as usual; but it was the first time he had asked me to do anything like that. When I took the envelope to the Igaya that afternoon, Seiko Nēsan looked startled at first, but quickly recovered her composure and thanked me profusely as she opened a bottle of beer. Then she said, "You've been to a hospital, haven't you?" She had noticed that the gauze dressing on my face was different from the one she had seen the other day. I was using the medication and gauze Dr. Harada had given me, instead of what I'd bought at the pharmacy.

"Sorry to worry you."

"There's a lot of mean characters around here, you know. Watch out, and don't let looks fool you."

Seiko Nēsan still seemed convinced that I had been beaten up by one of the local toughs. Bandages and gauze might all seem alike, but there are subtle differences, and this woman was definitely the kind who didn't miss such small distinctions.

As I was walking along a busy shopping street on my way back, I saw two or three cheap gangster types coming out of the glass doors of a building. Aya-chan came out right behind, and after catching up to them she walked on past me. I recognized one of the men who came out first as the one who had come to my apartment and told me he was Aya-chan's brother. I could tell at a glance that he seemed to be the leader among the three. I had no intention of tracking them, but it would look that way if I kept on going, so I stopped and stood staring into a shop window at a stuffed animal that resembled some kind of monstrous horse. The four of them went into a coffee shop, and that was the end of it.

I walked on. The encounter left me shaken, however,

like having unexpectedly come across a snake in my path someplace.

I decided to do something desperate, like jumping off a cliff. No, that's an exaggeration; I would play decoy and test people's reactions. I just had to do *something*, anything, to expose myself to others. I stepped into the phone booth in front of the train station on my way to lunch and flipped the pages of the directory, more or less pretending to look up a number. I put in a coin and dialed at random; a young woman answered the phone.

"Uh, hello? It's me. I'm a little boy's mummy."

"I beg your pardon?"

"I'm the mummy of a little boy from ancient times."

"Mama! There's somebody on the phone saying weird things!"

She hung up. *So there*, I thought; but then, as I left the booth, I was struck by an overwhelming feeling of self-loathing. Yes, I was "somebody saying weird things." The dull, oily sunlight of a late June day splashed across my face.

Later, Seiko Nēsan came by to see me.

"The swelling hasn't gone away yet, has it?" she said. I was braced for more, but she didn't say anything else. She took a piece of paper out of her handbag and began poring over something penciled on it. From what I could see, it looked like an array of random numbers. She also took out a small notebook and began scribbling something in it with a stubby pencil. When she had finished and put it all away, she said, "You don't seem to play the horses or go to the boat races. Just what do you do for fun?"

"I don't need to do anything in particular for fun."

"Don't need—?" Seiko Nēsan quit talking. I could see a vein

standing out on her temple. She might have thought I was insulting her. After that, she smoked her cigarette for a while as usual and left. Today was the first time, though, that she had pulled out a paper with those numbers or the little notebook. I wondered if she had let down her guard for a moment, or if she had done it deliberately. What was that vein on her temple all about?

The next morning, Sai-chan had no sooner left than I had another visitor. It was the man who had been standing with his hand in his pocket that day in the alley next to the apartment building.

"My name's Sōda. Sorry you had to go to all that trouble the other day."

"Oh?"

"Didn't mean to bother you so early in the morning, too, but . . . " He was speaking in the local dialect, but had a slight north-country accent. He had his hand in his pocket this morning, too, just like the other day.

"Is there something I can do for you?"

"Well, Miss Kishida's done me some favors, too, so it's kind of hard for me to say this, but listen: when you need a public phone, well, you know the phone booth in front of the train station? Would you mind using a different one?" He looked me in the eyes for the first time. "I hate to bring this up, really, but—see, there's been a lot of people watching you ever since." He didn't take his eyes off mine. His look told me that he clearly knew my call had been a charade.

"Uh, yes, I understand. Well . . . "

"Good. Thanks. I didn't really want to have to do this." He looked around the room out of the corner of his eye. "Well, have a nice day."

After he left, I felt a cold sweat breaking out all over my body. It was perfectly clear to me now that this man with his hand in his pocket had associates who were watching me all the time. I suspected that it was not so much out of concern for me that he had brought this up, but rather to warn me to stay out of the way. At the same time he seemed to be assuring me that I wouldn't suffer any harm as long as I didn't make any more stupid moves, but what he said also contained a hint that others— members of some rival gang, maybe—might be watching me. If so, it could mean trouble for me at any time.

Did this mean I really had pushed myself off the cliff? It was a sign of my situation here that it took this visit from Sōda for me to learn that Seiko Nēsan's family name was Kishida.

Sai-chan came by that evening as if nothing had happened. Was he just dumb, or was he being an ass? I had known this was his style all along; it was somehow irritating, but I went on and handed him the processed meat as if nothing were the matter.

There was a thunderstorm that night. Thunder rumbled across the sky; lightning flashed; every so often, a huge clap of thunder accompanied a bolt that struck the earth. Suddenly a man and woman came upstairs, babbling unintelligibly, and dashed into the apartment next door. They talked and made noise for a while, then things got quiet; I assumed they had begun their lovemaking. I couldn't hear the usual incantations over the noise of the storm, and that spurred my imagination. With unusual clarity, I visualized a beautiful picture of the two of them coupling in that cheap apartment, their limbs entwined as the thunder roared outside and lightning lit up the window panes.

13

I began to look around myself more carefully after the man with his hand in his pocket came by. Since I arrived in Amagasaki, I'd used the public phone once when I first called the Igaya, then again when I called before going to Dr. Harada's, and then once more the time I made that fake call. That was all. I thought for a moment about going to another phone booth and flipping through the directories there, but I knew that things wouldn't go well with me this time if I did anything so foolish.

While eating *gyōza* dumplings and rice at a Chinese restaurant in the neighborhood, I overheard some of the other customers talking. They were discussing a recent incident in which a group of taxi drivers had taken to knocking off work early so they could gamble at a mah-jongg parlor, leaving nine cabs lined up on a back street. When they left the gambling den after it was time to return to the garage, they discovered that every one of the cabs was gone. Evidently a neighborhood woman, exasperated by seeing a line of cabs parked on her street day after day, had called the police; the vehicles had all been towed off, and the drivers had gone back to their offices shamefaced and empty-handed. Having gambled since morning, they of course had made no fares and had to face some pretty harsh music.

Despite such experiences, this crowd showed no signs of straightening up. Showing up at work in the morning, they would go straight to gamble at the horse or bicycle track, the boat races or motorcycle races, a mah-jongg joint or *pachinko* pinball parlor; in between, they might also call an illicit bookie joint to bet money they could ill afford to lose on the horses or baseball games. When time came to knock off, they usually went back flat broke and turned in debt vouchers for the fares they should have earned; so it went, day after day. Come payday, what ought to have been three hundred fifty thousand yen or more ended up reduced to two or three thousand, and they had no choice but to go back to the same habits for the next month. The taxi companies couldn't afford to fire them, however. They wouldn't have enough staff if they kept firing the delinquent drivers, who were all already in debt to the company in a big way. The drivers, who were very much aware of this of course, kept right on going to the mah-jongg parlors and boat races as soon as they showed up for duty; apparently, some portion of every taxi company's force was like this.

I was sure this was another case of desperate lives, oil oozing from assholes. These people were at a raw edge between despair and pleasure, feeling they would suffocate without the release they got from gambling. Carrying on such a life, as if possessed by demons, told me that they were already among the living dead; in this example I saw the epitome of life without substance.

No one would live this way if he had the choice, of course. The man who came by my place with his hand in his pocket the other day might very well have been one of those who made illicit book on the races or baseball games. The number chart Seiko Nēsan had been looking over was probably connected with this business in some way. Sai-chan's strangely taciturn affect was a strong enough hint that his life, too, concealed deep secrets within. Being involved in the drug trade was no doubt associated with some unspoken setback in his life, something he could not escape. For certain, his customers were even worse off. It was unfortunate, of course, but an ill wind prevails in this society, blowing people in this unfortunate direction. Likewise, I didn't doubt that the kind who hit the mah-jongg parlors and racetracks first thing in the morning were caught up in these same fierce currents, not caring what would come next. The same tempest had been blowing within me as I drifted, from Tokyo to Himeji, Kyoto, Kobe, Nishinomiya, and finally here to "Ama."

The first of July was my thirty-fourth birthday, but I had no particular hopes or fervent wishes. I was born in the summer of the final year of the war, the year of total defeat. My father was planting rice as B-29 bombers flew overhead, and someone brought him news from home that a boy had been born. The overcast sky was reflected in the waters of the flooded rice paddy; I remember him telling me the story. Now I was four years older than he was at that time.

The woman with the reddish hair was visiting across the hall again. She seemed to be about my age: that is, she seemed to have put in about as much time on this earth as I had. I'm sure she had thought long and hard, and was seeking to recover from some deep despair, to have come this far and now be wearing a tattoo all over her back. Overhearing her anguished groans, I sensed that mere words were insignificant when it came to agitating the human mind. I had no idea what sort of painful karma had her in its grip, but her raw outcries struck my ears as an unmistakable supplication for life.

All I did day after day, though, was cut up beef and pork organs and stick them on skewers. Sooner or later they would wind up in someone's mouth, be digested inside his organs, and vanish into the toilet as excrement. I wasn't sure what happened after that, but I assumed the residue would eventually be washed out into the ocean. It was just the same with the glamorous goods lining the shelves in the department stores and supermarkets; someday they would all become rubbish or shit. This was the essence of all human activity; this was why I could tell Seiko Nēsan in all honesty that I had no particular need for pleasurable pursuits.

Late one night, I ran into Aya-chan when I went to buy a cold beer out of the vending machine in front of the local liquor store. There was nothing more to it than that, but I let slip a cry of surprise. Aya-chan glared at me.

"What the hell do you want?" she said.

She had just come from the public baths, and her hair, still wet, was glistening; her bra and tattoo showed through her white blouse. She could tell that I had noticed.

"You need to quit just looking if you want to get a thrill out of a woman, honey."

"What?" The words cut me to the heart. She shot me a knowing smile.

"That's what makes me sick about you. You don't understand, do you?" She smiled again, and there was some hidden meaning behind the smile. "Well, look all you want, but I don't want the dirt in your mind coming off on me, you know—here I am, just now all cleaned up. Hey, your face's a lot better now, isn't it?"

Her body gave off the fragrance of soap. *Then she pulled up her skirt and jumped, like this . . .*

"What kind of look is that?"

"Ah . . . oh, thank you for the cherries the other day."

"Good, weren't they?"

"Yes." I couldn't very well tell her that I hadn't really enjoyed eating them.

"Horimayu-san said to take you some, too."

"What?"

"Why do you get so shook up all the time?"

"Oh, no—"

"Are you getting me wrong some kind of way because of what I said?"

"Well, no, I—"

"'I' what?"

I was at a loss for what to say.

"You're not going to make it here, Mister Ikushima. You're not like us."

Aya-chan put money in the vending machine. As she stooped to get the can of beer that dropped out, I saw the tattoo through her blouse again. After picking up the can, she walked off without looking at me.

Drinking beer out of the can alone in my apartment, I told myself that I wanted to stick it out here as long as I could. I figured that Aya-chan was doing the same thing downstairs, drinking cold beer out of the can, maybe looking up at the ceiling and thinking back on how she ran into that guy Ikushima a while ago in front of the liquor store. No, I was kidding myself. She had backed this Ikushima type into a corner, until he was speechless. Judging from how she walked off coolly without so much as a glance back at me, she was more than likely enjoying her after-bath beer without another thought. She was that kind of woman.

Aya-chan had me nailed from the start. I had cut a pretty sorry figure, not able to get out so much as a coherent word. I'd been fooling myself, assuming that Gō-chan had told on me; she had probably noticed herself that I was tailing her that day. On the other hand, it was natural to think that Horimayu-san had just happened to suggest bringing me the cherries. In any case, it was a fact that she had shocked me with her remarks that afternoon, so much that I could hardly taste the cherries. And again tonight the words had been a rock in my gut: *You need to quit just looking if you want to get a thrill out of a woman.* The tattoo that showed through her blouse looked like a great bird with its wings outspread, just as Shimpei had said.

Whatever, it was disturbing to have *chanced to see.* I had seen the toad in the bottom of the pipe again. The empty beer can spurred my thirst; I sat there with my shoulders heaving, breathing heavily as the rain outside began to spatter on the window.

14

One afternoon, Shimpei came into my apartment shouting "Bloody cock! Bloody cock!" at the top of his voice. Seeing my surprised look, he told me, "It's OK, Mister. It's just a thing going around our school right now. Everybody's yelling 'Bloody cock.'"

"Oh, I see."

"See, like this: 'Bloody cock! Bloody cock!' They all run around yelling it out loud. If you remember 'Bloody cock' for four years, you die."

"What?"

"That's why Miss Fujie gets mad when we say 'Bloody cock.' She makes a face like this—a funny face, like this." Shimpei's eyes looked as if they had suddenly gone completely out of focus. "So everybody starts running around again, yelling 'Bloody cock! Bloody cock!' Sumiko-chan does it. Ton-chan does it. It's fun."

After blurting out all this as if delirious, Shimpei ran out the door. Some sort of bizarre mass hysteria seemed to be afoot. Unexpectedly, Horimayu-san's face peeked around the door.

"Say, Ikushima my friend, got a minute?"

I stood up out of the chair. "Sure. Please come on in."

He walked in unhurriedly and glanced around the room. I hastily washed my hands. He stayed standing in the entry, just inside the door.

"Actually, I need you to do me a favor."

"What can I do for you?"

As usual, his eyes were bloodshot. I approached him, wondering how to refuse if the favor were something I couldn't possibly perform.

"It's nothing, really. I just need you to keep this at your place for two, three days." He held out a package about the size of a small candy box, wrapped in paper and neatly tied with twine. I hesitated for a second, but there was no way I could refuse after he had thrust it at me with that fearsome look in his eyes. In my hand, it felt heavier than its looks suggested.

"Is it all right if I keep it in the closet?"

"Sure. Well, thanks."

Horimayu-san left. I held the box in both hands and shook it; I could faintly hear something moving inside but couldn't imagine what it might be. I was certain, at least, that this was something he couldn't keep in his apartment downstairs or in his workroom up here or entrust to some other individual he knew. Horimayu-san had given me custody of some secret— or rather, he had made me a kind of partner in it. As I put it in the closet, it occurred to me that I should have told him about the broken latch on my front door. Thinking about those eyes, however, I didn't feel comfortable going downstairs to tell him.

Seiko Nēsan came by. She hadn't been in for a while since that time the vein popped out on her temple. I had wondered how she was doing, but had left her alone since I had made it a rule not to make any unprompted overtures toward her. Coming in without a word as usual, she sat down, heaved a sigh, and began fiddling with a bandage covering the end of her left middle finger.

"Look at me—Now I'm cutting myself with a kitchen knife, too."

"How did that happen?"

"Oh, no big deal. Looks like your face's pretty much back to normal, but I bet you'll have a scar."

"Stuff happens."

"When I was walking past the market just now, I saw them selling these and bought you one." She opened a paper-wrapped bundle and took out a bonsai—a miniature zelkova tree.

"What do you think? Pretty, huh?"

"It sure is."

"How about taking care of it for me here at your place?"

"Oh—me? I'm afraid it won't get any sun in here."

"Bonsai plants actually do better without a lot of sun. You can put it over there in the window by the sink."

She stood up and put the plant on the sill of the bay window herself. As she did that, I caught a glimpse of the design on the wrapping paper. The name and address of the nursery were printed on it; it was no ordinary place near the markets. She must have bought it for me after thinking about what I had said—"I don't particularly need to do anything for fun." I felt a little pang of emotion when I realized this, but it wasn't going to be easy to keep this plant alive in this apartment. The pot was about the size of my hand, and the little tree was about four inches tall.

"Oh, it's no problem. Just give it a little water every day. Hell, it won't matter if it does go ahead and die."

"Well, then, thank you."

She then took two navel oranges out of her bag, both of them beautifully colored.

Three days passed, then five, but Horimayu-san didn't come for his box.

15

On one of my days off, I took the Hanshin train to Himejima Station and walked up onto the levee along the Yodo River. Back when I lived in Tokyo, I had sometimes taken walks along the Edo River to its mouth. Reeds grew thick; abandoned wooden boats sat stuck in the bottom mud; you could hear the cries of sandpipers and reed warblers, and flocks of white seagulls flew along the water's edge. Many wooden craft had been left to rot among the reeds, having been largely replaced by boats made from petrochemical resins. The bright green leaves of the fresh reeds, and the dry brown of the dead ones—the colors of both made a vivid impression on me as they swayed in the wind. I had seen no such color in the Yodo River scenery out of the windows of the train, but I still wanted to walk along the waterside road to the river's mouth.

On the opposite bank of the river was Konohana-Dempōchō, part of the city of Osaka, where small steel fabricator's shops and scrap-metal yards jostled beside polluted canals; to the south you could see rows of apartment blocks, high-voltage transmission towers, and the gas company's enormous storage tanks. It was much the same in the Himejima district on the near bank: factories belonging to miscellaneous small-scale enterprises were lined up along the levee, and huge steel mills came into view as I neared the mouth of the river. Marsh reeds had flourished in this area in the distant past, of course, but modern human beings, possessed by industrial rationalism, had made it their pleasure to replace the colors of the reeds with the gray of concrete. Such is the inevitable, irreversible flow of history.

I walked down onto the dry riverbed. The merciless July sun burned like a pale blue flame. Approaching the mouth of the river, I saw people here and there with fishing lines in the water. I had a nagging fear that the little box in the closet might disappear while I was away from my apartment.

I asked a father-and-son pair that I met, "What are they catching?"

"That's stupid. You think you could catch anything around here?" was the boy's reply.

There was a steel mill at the mouth of the river, its bizarre-looking dust collectors towering into the air. I walked past the end of its fence and came out onto a wide-open stretch of reclaimed land; it must have extended over eighty acres. Tall goldenrod covered the whole expanse except for the yellow blossom of an evening primrose now and again. There was no sign of people anywhere in this wasteland under the blinding sun. I walked through the weeds amid the sound of singing insects. The smell of the steaming hot foliage was stifling. I came across an abandoned car buried among the weeds; the wrecked vehicle was covered in a psychedelic pattern of red, blue, and yellow paint. Through the tall weeds I suddenly caught sight of Osaka Bay, its waters glittering in the three-o'clock summer light.

The sky was glowing red in the west as I started home. I

saw people fishing from the levee again but didn't notice them catching anything during the considerable time I spent watching. Nobody was talking, either. The only movement was the water of the river, reflecting the glow of the evening sun. I'm sure the people sitting there were hoping to catch something— anything, just something. Some would probably go home empty-handed, but to them a day without a catch was probably no different from a successful one. It was just another day of life, like the one I'd spent coming here.

That night, I was sitting on the tatami floor reading the newspaper I had bought at the train station when I heard the door open quietly behind me. I turned around. I saw Aya-chan already in the entry, closing the door behind her. As usual, the latch fell off when the door closed. She tried to put it back but gave up when she saw that it was broken; she turned, looked at me, and came on in. I sensed that something out of the ordinary was happening when I realized that she was not taking her eyes off me. I swallowed hard.

She was standing there barefooted, watching me without saying a word. I was sitting on the tatami with one knee propped up; I turned my head to look at her but froze where I sat. She suddenly reached down and thrust her hands into the skirts of her dress. The fabric fluttered up loosely. She reached up to her hips and pulled her panties down in one quick motion and then looked straight at me. The panties hung around her calves. First she slipped them off her raised right foot, then did the same with the left; she picked them up and thrust them out toward me, pinched in the fingers of her right hand. Without taking her eyes off me, she threw the panties onto the newspaper in front of me. I glanced at them and looked at her. She was standing there with her hands hanging loosely at her sides, watching me steadily with narrowed eyes, as if biting the inside of her lip. After a little while, she reached around behind her back, unhooked the top of her dress, and pulled the zipper down to her waist in a single move. She kept her eyes on me the whole time.

I felt myself drawing in a startled breath. She reached up toward the hanging light bulb switch, and the room went dark. The white dress fell around her feet. A tiny sliver of light came in from the slightly open door. Her eyes were still on me.

"Stand up," she said. As I obeyed, I could see her pale, naked body approaching me. She pulled my polo shirt up and off over my head; unfastening my belt buckle and reaching abruptly into my shorts, she grasped my penis and testicles with one hand. A shiver ran through my body. She kept her hand there for a while, loosening and tightening her grip, looking into my eyes the whole time. Withdrawing her hand, she unzipped my slacks and pulled them down along with my shorts. She would have had them down in one swift move, but my erection was already in the way. She leaned over and pulled harder; I put my hand on her shoulder and struggled to free the trousers and underwear from around my ankles. Between the tangled strands of hair around her shoulders I caught a glimpse of the tattoo on her back, glistening in the dark like the scales on a snake. Once my trousers and underwear were out of the way, she looked up at me as she sank down to her knees. She took my penis in one hand and began to caress it between her lips. Every cell in my body was trembling. Standing up, she turned her back toward me and said, "Unhook me."

I could see that the tattoo covered her entire back, though in the dark I couldn't make out the design. I pictured Horimayu-san's bloodshot eyes in the darkness. I loosened the hooks of her bra with trembling fingers; it fell to the floor as I touched the straps, and I reached around her as I stood there. I kissed her around the ears; when I grasped her breasts with both hands and pinched her nipples in my fingers, she let out a little cry. At the same time, she flung my hands off and turned around. That raptor-like look returned to her eyes for a moment as she gripped me in a fierce embrace. We kissed as though we had both lost our senses, our male and female animal spirits flaming up as hot tongue uncontrollably sought hot tongue. The pounding of her heart reverberated against my chest; I was sure that she could feel the throbbing of my pulse as well. The summer sunlight glittering on Osaka Bay flashed across my mind. We were male and female beasts, our souls bleeding, driven now by instinct alone. The strength went out of my knees, and we collapsed together like a wall of melting ice. In the darkness, it felt as though the world were coming to an end.

16

It had been raining all morning. This was the fourth day in a row that it had rained without a stop, after a short break in the summer rainy season. I had been chopping up organ meats, hardly stopping to take a breath, well before Sai-chan was due to arrive that morning. It was impossible for me to stay in the apartment any more without doing something—anything. If I just sat there, every breath I took was unbearably painful. Putting up with that stifling, unbearable feeling, though, was all that life had become for me now. I thought about Horimayu-san's eyes, and I thought about the little box. If worse came to worst I was prepared to cut off the end of one of my fingers to make amends, as the gangsters did, but I wasn't sure if that would be enough. Still, I couldn't make up my mind to leave; I had nowhere to go.

After our violent, passionate lovemaking that night five days before, Aya-chan sat there for a long time in the darkness, silently, with her bare breasts outthrust. After a while, she got dressed—still in the dark—and left without saying a word. I said nothing, either, as I watched her go; I couldn't speak—or rather, something was dead inside me where words should have been formed; it was as though my entire psyche had been burned to ashes. I had ejaculated five times in a row, without a break. The first three were frenzied shots, never withdrawing; Aya-chan let me come in her mouth the last two times. It was pure heaven on earth, but by the same token each ejaculation was also a moment of death. During that vile, empty time following those ejaculations, I lay there like a corpse, my shriveled member dangling and limp.

Aya-chan's white panties were still there. Whether she had left them on purpose, or if she had forgotten them, I didn't know. I wrapped them up in a newspaper in the dark and was about to put them in the closet when my hand happened to touch that box. Changing my mind, I decided to put them in the refrigerator instead. As I opened the refrigerator door, the glare of the light bulb almost blinded me and the reek of raw organs assailed my nostrils. At the same moment, it occurred to me that in the dark I hadn't been able to get a good look at Aya-chan's tattoo. Silently I cursed myself. I remembered distinctly that the design looked like some kind of big bird with outspread wings, but I hadn't been able to make out anything more. The two oranges that Seiko Nēsan had left the other day were lying in the refrigerator, their colors still bright. I put the newspaper bundle away in the vegetable crisper at the bottom and closed the door.

And so deceitful *words*—that product of the human mind—began to arise in me again. I hadn't seen Aya-chan since that night. I tried to spy on her unnoticed, but I saw nothing of her. Once, as I was walking along the downstairs hallway toward Aya-chan's apartment, the door of the unit right in front of me suddenly jerked open. An old man came out; he was the one I had seen picking through garbage back in May. Looking at me, he said, "You want something?"

"No, actually—"

Feeling myself going pale, I turned my back on him. I had made a blunder. As I was cutting up meat and sticking it on skewers in grim silence, that feeling came over me again: the shiver I had felt when Aya-chan suddenly grasped my cock and balls.

From out in the corridor, eyes were watching me through the slightly open door. The eyes belonged to Shimpei. I had noticed but pretended not to be aware. He didn't just open the door and come into the apartment, as he usually did; he must have sensed that something out of the ordinary was going on with me. If so, then I somehow needed to shake it off. He kept staring at me; why wouldn't he come in? I began to feel tense. I feared the something extraordinary that seemed to have come over me. I wanted to call out to him, "Shimpei-chan!" but the words wouldn't come.

Suddenly, I heard him cry "Aw!" and there was a noise of something like marbles scattering over the floor. I could tell that he was out there picking them up, one by one.

17

I ran into Horimayu-san in the alley next to the apartment house. Neither of us could see the other's face since both of us were carrying umbrellas, but I felt every cell in my body tense up as though frozen solid; I stopped. The chance result was that I yielded the way to him. If I hadn't, he might have sensed something different about me, just as Shimpei had the day before. Even after I got out into the main street, the oppressive feeling in my chest didn't go away. I wondered why Horimayu-san hadn't come to take back the box he had left in my care. If he came, though, I knew our eyes would have to meet. I couldn't forget the bloodshot whites of his eyes from the time I saw him in the darkness six days before.

In the middle of the night, I impulsively took the two oranges out of the refrigerator and wolfed them down. The sweet juice dripped from the edges of my mouth. After I finished eating, I sat there with my back against the refrigerator door as if in a trance. As I sat there with my legs sprawled out, Aya-chan came, naked, and wrapped herself around me. My penis swelled until it was bigger than the rest of my body.

That woman was back in the apartment across the hall,

groaning once again. Horimayu-san was no doubt plying his needle, his eyes bloodshot, his back teeth clenched. I no longer felt any of my initial intense curiosity, however, even though I could visualize the scene and hear the woman's voice. Aya-chan's moans, panting, and cries of pleasure in the midst of our lovemaking were still reverberating in my head. When Aya-chan spread her genitals wide and told me "Do it," I sucked and licked them like a desperate man. I trembled as I did it; it aroused fears in me of being killed. Even as that fear gripped me, though, I couldn't keep from going on, sucking and licking to my heart's content as if the world were about to end. Compared to that drowning-like feeling of passion and premonition of death, the noises the woman was making across the hall seemed very distant now. I was concerned that I hadn't seen any sign of Aya-chan since; then again, I was apprehensive about getting another sudden visit, yet I couldn't deny the desire to grasp her soft breasts again. While that red-haired woman was across the hall it was not going to happen; from that point of view, the agonized groans that should have sounded like someone about to die were actually a source of comfort.

The rainy season ended. The summer sun, intense already from early in the morning on, beat down on the earth below. The shadows of the houses were darker now; the leaves glittered brightly on the tall trees. I walked down Teramachi, the street that ran along the south side of the Hanshin Railway tracks. Trespassing on the grounds of a temple, I sat down on a stone in the shadow of a tree. It was not much of a temple, being in the middle of town, but it had its own cemetery, with perhaps 150 stones—a multitude of spirits, congregating at an eternal banquet of lights. There were centuries-old graves from the feudal days, of people who had lived their lives to the full as well as those who had died young, of those who had succumbed to disease, accidents, or violence; all of them were here at their summer banquet, their attachments still strong to the one life we are each allotted. Aya-chan had come to visit at night on my previous day off, and I hadn't seen her since; I wondered what she was doing. Thinking about it had been making me restless; sitting here now in the shade among the banqueting spirits gave me some relief. I, too, was living my one allotted life.

Aya-chan didn't say a single word that night to reveal her thoughts. It was puzzling enough that she had come upstairs without warning like that; she was usually so direct about expressing her feelings, but she said nothing of the kind either during our lovemaking or afterward.

I was worried. The wordless, even deathly silence that followed in the darkness after our encounter might not just have been the result of having spent our energies in sex. Her appearing upstairs without warning, first, and then her not having been seen since, made me think there might be something seriously wrong going on. The mad, passionate way she made love to me had the all the marks of desperation. It worried me more and more every time I thought about it. Still, I continued to see Horimayu-san and Shimpei from time to time as if nothing had changed, so there didn't seem to be much reason to say anything. Maybe she had gone to see her brother. But there was no way to be sure of that, and I couldn't bring myself to question Shimpei about it either.

I left the temple grounds and walked southward along the river toward the steel mills and iron works. There was a reek of concrete, rusty iron, oil, chemicals, and smoke; the weeds along the road were thickly coated with dust. I didn't see any of the big trucks that usually roared by, or any sign of people. I was seized by the desire to see the tattoo on Aya-chan's back again, only this time in the light. Horimayu-san must surely have injected his very soul into the needle as he executed that tattoo. That was how the man with the bloodshot eyes spoke his *words*, and that's why I was so obsessed with seeing it again. I wanted to take Aya-chan from behind, like a dog, and fondle her generous breasts while I stared down at that tattoo.

What a brutal kind of thirst this carnal desire was. It was making me irrational, and I was afraid. The nagging, trembling fear that the box might vanish while I was away from my apartment was my ever-present companion. Why hadn't Horimayu-san come to get it? My real thirst kept getting worse as I walked aimlessly through the factory district that Sunday afternoon. I looked around for a vending machine that sold drinks, but saw none.

Seiko Nēsan came by. She sat there smoking, as usual, for a while. After crushing the cigarette out in the empty tin can I used for an ashtray, she looked straight at me and spoke: "I heard you stalked Aya-chan a while back."

She must have noticed the change in my expression.

"Yep, I heard right. Gō-chan came by last night for a drink and told me."

I was speechless.

"You do stuff like that because you don't know how dangerous a guy Horimayu-san is. Didn't I tell you, when you first got here, not to mess with that girl?"

I stayed silent.

"So why do you do stupid stuff like that? Sure, Aya-chan's a hot little number; she could make a guy's balls sing a tune. But listen: she's—" She abruptly stopped talking. A bluish vein was standing out on her temple.

"I'm very sorry." I said, and bowed my head. The blue vein must have been a sign of jealousy. Aya-chan's panties were still in my refrigerator, cold.

"Listen, honey, I know it's no fun sticking chicken on skewers day after day in a place like this. But Aya-chan—well, she doesn't know this yet, either, but—"

Every nerve ending in my body was raw as I waited to hear her next words. Seiko Nēsan glanced toward the refrigerator.

"—No, I'd better not tell you about it. But listen to me: don't you ever do anything like that again, you understand? You'll wind up dead."

"I'm really sorry about what I did."

"I've put the word to Gō-chan, so it's all right. Listen: you understand now, don't you? There's no ifs, ands, or buts. You promise me?"

"Yes, ma'am. Sorry I caused you a problem."

But Seiko Nēsan had let something slip. I didn't know what she had been about to say, of course, but her harried tone of voice was a sign that something wasn't right. I could tell she wasn't just speaking out of jealousy. She wasn't taking me to task for my foolishness just out of concern for my safety, either; there was something ominous on her mind. Definitely, my apprehensions had not been groundless. It was clear that Aya-chan's recent disappearance meant something serious. She might not know it yet, but her own life might be in danger. No, events were already afoot that made danger certain. Seiko Nēsan knew it, and she knew that I, too, would be dead if she made me a party to it.

Surely Aya-chan already knew what was happening. That unannounced visit; the heavy breathing in the darkness; the kisses; the trembling and shaking; the desperate caressing of my member; the leaden silence after the act; her breasts out-thrust; the forgotten panties—wasn't all that evidence? Speaking hardly a word the whole time, she had simply consumed my soul like a flame. What I took for dull silence on her part was really a desperate forbearance; she must have been fearful for my safety.

I wondered what Gō-chan had told Seiko Nēsan, and in what fashion. Had he told Horimayu-san, too? Probably. If so, was it that afternoon when Aya-chan brought up the bowl of cherries, or was it afterward? Why had Horimayu-san said, "Take him some cherries, too"? What did he mean when he said, "So that clown brought the bowl back empty? He's a piece of work"? Most of all, what had happened to Aya-chan? I tried to get back to work after Seiko Nēsan left, but my mind was in such turmoil I couldn't start up again.

However great the turmoil in one's mind, with time it eventually settles down. More important in getting me back to work was the knowledge that Sai-chan would not fail to come that evening. After he came and left, I went out to the empty lot in back for a breath of fresh air, but I found only the still, sultry atmosphere of a summer evening. The dead toad was gone. Going back in after sitting on one of the clay drainpipes for a while, I encountered Horimayu-san again; the image of the one-eyed chicken flashed through my mind. He just glanced at me and walked past.

I looked to one side and happened to see Aya-chan about to lock her apartment door. She shot a look at me; for a second, I could see her eyes moving in the dim light at the end of the corridor. I held my breath. She just came toward me, however, looking in my direction as if nothing had happened. I stood stock-still, listening to the violent pounding of my pulse. She walked by in front of me, as though giving a stranger some extra space, and went on. Still facing the dimly lit depths of the corridor, I couldn't even turn around to see her as she walked away.

18

After that, Aya-chan seemed to settle back in downstairs. She wasn't a model homemaker; I often saw empty meal-delivery containers outside her door. The next time I saw her was also downstairs, while she was talking to a woman who had come to pick up a container from an earlier delivery. Our eyes met over the woman's shoulder, but there was no particular reaction on Aya-chan's part, and I couldn't very well just stand there. I went back upstairs to my apartment and waited tensely for a while, as though something would happen, but nothing did.

From then on I began to catch sight of Aya-chan occasionally. The only time she gave any indication of her inner thoughts, though, had been that once in the hallway when I caught the expression in her eyes; we had hardly exchanged a word since then, much less had anything more serious to do with each other. I thought I detected a certain stiffness in her manner when our eyes happened to meet, but for the most part she treated me like a complete stranger. It wasn't like her to be that way, of course, but I was sure she had a purpose in it. Being conscious of that, I did my best to stay away from her as well. I suppressed my pent-up desire, keeping my head down to avoid looking at her–what's more, I was afraid that Horimayu-san would suspect something if he caught me eyeing her.

Something else was bothering me: that foreboding I had felt when Seiko Nēsan came to visit the other day. I concentrated every nerve in my body on catching the slightest change in Aya-chan's behavior, but she showed no sign; that could mean she really was completely unaware, just as Seiko Nēsan had said. Of course, Seiko Nēsan herself hadn't said anything more to me about that since her visit. Being who she was, though, I could tell she was quietly keeping a sharp eye on me, all the while acting as though nothing was the matter.

As the days passed, the events of the earlier night began to feel as if they had been no more than scenes in a bad dream. Still, something unexpected could happen again anytime, without warning, just like that. What was Aya-chan thinking when she came upstairs that night? Was she feeling sorry for me? Was she attracted to me? Surely not. I feared the "barefooted woman" lurking within her. Her panties were still there, cold, in my refrigerator.

Staring blankly into space while leaning against that refrigerator in the hot July night, I began to recall summers during high school when I ran madly across hills and fields, hunting the butterflies that were my obsession at the time. I sublimated my solitude in the pursuit of those beautiful insects; the moment I caught a chestnut tiger in my white net on a mountainside one summer, I felt as if I were walking on air. I got a kind of necromaniac's pleasure out of displaying my mounted specimens in glass cases. While I was wrapped up in my memories, I suddenly began to hear those weird incantations again coming out of the apartment next door. I knew that a couple had gone in there a while before; it had been several weeks, though, since the chanting woman had been there. Thinking about lovemaking with Aya-chan, I whispered the meaningless phrases along with her.

Shimpei was standing forlornly at the entry to the alley. When he saw me, he started talking with a miserable look in his eyes.

"Mister . . . you know what I did? I messed up all the origami things Sumiko-chan made for me."

"What? How?"

"Yeah, well, I spilled tea all over 'em. I tried to dry 'em, but Mr. Rabbit and Mr. Crocodile got all messed up, like this."

He took Mr. Rabbit and Mr. Crocodile out of his pocket and showed them to me. The colors had run, and the legs wilted.

In August, the heat got even worse. The apartment reeked of spoiled organ meat. Horimayu-san seemed to be in the apartment across the hall during the afternoons, but I couldn't tell if he was working or not. I summoned up the courage to knock on his door; no answer. I knocked again. The door suddenly opened, and Horimayu-san stuck out his face. "What do you want?" He had the same terrible look in his eyes.

"Uh, it's about that box I've been keeping for you for a while now."

"Yeah? What about it?"

"I was worried that I hadn't heard from you about it since."

"It's important."

"In that case . . . ?"

"Sorry, but I need you to keep it a while longer. I've got my reasons."

"But if it's important, that's all the more reason for me to be concerned."

"I asked you to keep it because it's something I can't replace, you see?"

"But I . . . "

"Seems to me I gave you ten thousand yen at the station."

I was becoming agitated.

"But I'm starting to think that wasn't enough."

"Being as it's so important, would you mind telling me what's in the box? "

"Why do you want to know?"

He kept his eyes on me for a while, staring fiercely. A trickle of sweat went down my cheek.

"You've gotten buddy-buddy with my boy Shimpei, haven't you?"

I suddenly remembered him shouting "Bullshit!" at me.

"What the hell's that all about? You got your sights on Ayako next?"

I was speechless.

"You can have her if you want. I've seen you checking her out."

"Well, no, I—"

"'I' what? You trying to tell me you're in love with her, maybe? She goes on about 'Ikushima-san' all the time, you know; she's got the hots for you, bad."

I was even more tongue-tied than before.

"I—uh—all I wanted to do was ask about that box I'm keep-ing for you."

"Like I said before, do me a favor—I need you to keep it just a little longer."

"All right—how long do you think it'll be?"

"Ikushima, my friend, do you really have to have everything nailed down like that? Don't you understand? I've asked you to do this because there's some things I can't explain right now, even if I wanted to. From the first time I saw you at Ama Station, I thought you were a guy I could depend on."

"No, I'm really not worth a damn."

"Maybe so, but Ayako keeps talking about 'Ikushima-san, Ikushima-san.'"

"Uh—" I was in a hurry to wind up this conversation, but at the same time I desperately wanted him to tell me more about Aya-chan.

"Listen, buddy: how about taking Ayako on for me? She's pining away for you."

Really? I almost let the word slip out. He was clearly teasing me now: it was a trap.

"The lock on my apartment door's broken. I don't think it's a safe place to keep something important." I said.

"You expecting a visit from a burglar?"

"You never know what might happen."

"Nah—you're a guy with a conscience. You'd make it up to me somehow if anything happened."

"No, I'm afraid a loser like me couldn't do anything in that situation; it would just be a problem for you, Horimayu-san."

"Wait a minute, bud, when did I say you could call me 'Horimayu-san'? Huh?"

"Oh, no, I'm sorry."

"So you're telling me you don't want to do me the favor?"

"No, no, of course not . . . "

"I hate to say it, but my own life's the only thing more important to me than that box. Here I am asking you now, man to man, to do me a favor and keep it for me. You telling me to kiss off?"

The conversation was going nowhere. "Well, I haven't told

anybody up till now about keeping the box for you. Would you mind if I asked Seiko Nēsan her advice about it?"

"No, not that old woman. The only thing keeping her alive is greed. She's not like you; she'd give in to curiosity about what's inside."

At that moment I had a flash of recognition: Horimayu-san might have given himself away. Entrusting the box to me might have been a snare from the very beginning. If so, its contents might not be so valuable after all. But I had no basis for this conclusion either.

"Ikushima-kun, you're not a selfish individual."

"Beg your pardon?"

"I've come to respect the way you work every day. I couldn't imagine doing a job like that, day in and day out, and for practically nothing."

"No, I'm just a . . . "

"Not only that. When you finish up for the day, you don't sit around watching TV; you don't gamble. No wonder Ayako's all shook up. She calls you 'the mummy of some ancient boy.'"

Again, I was speechless.

"Let me tell you: I've had some tough jobs, but I couldn't do what you do: shitty work like that, day after day. What the hell does the old bitch at the Igaya think she's doing, feeding people guts out of pigs and cows that got sick and died?"

I was growing impatient.

"Listen, bud—why don't you give Ayako's pussy a little rub for me sometime? It's itching for some attention. She's hot for you to do it, not me."

"Oh, no, I couldn't—"

"It's good and juicy." He kept his eyes steadily on me as he gave me a knowing leer. "I can't keep my mind on my work, you know."

"Uh—excuse me—I'd better be going now."

Horimayu-san had shown me that his words were a trap. In fact, he had set a double trap for me. The contents of his words were a trap, and his revealing them as a trap was itself a trap. Not only that: if he suspected that Aya-chan and I had already been intimate, that would be yet another, even more sinister trap. Furthermore, his arousing my curiosity about the contents of the box, and his remarks about respecting my attitude toward my work, were clearly deceptive enticements. To think that I had almost slipped and fallen for them—I could not help becoming even more fearful of the man.

In fact, I had seen for myself how frightening he could be. That incident with the chicken's eyes was enough. The immediate problem was the box he had left in my care. Originally I had just thought of it as an imposition, but I hadn't imagined it could be a trap. Then Aya-chan showed up out of nowhere, and there was that practically catastrophic encounter. The box was weighing more and more heavily on my mind, but I was such an idiot I had never suspected the box might be some kind of trap. Horimayu-san must have gotten the word somehow from Gō-chan, sensed a risk in the way I looked at Aya-chan before she came up to see me, then decided to watch and set me up for some kind of trouble by foisting that box on me.

For her part, maybe Aya-chan had caught on to what was going on. Maybe there had been some kind of altercation with Horimayu-san that ended up provoking her to action; it often happens. She had probably made up her mind that I was a soft touch and decided to burst in on me like that while

Horimayu-san and Shimpei were out. That had puckered me up severely, though it was also a moment of supreme delight.

But why had she come up? I absolutely couldn't believe it was only because of what Horimayu-san said—"she's pining away for you"—especially when I thought about the nearly insane intensity of her lovemaking. He was obviously leading me on when he said "She keeps talking about 'Ikushima-san, Ikushima-san'"—yet it was a tribute to the attraction I felt (it "could make a guy's balls sing a tune") that his words could make me want to hear more.

I wondered what would happen if Horimayu-san found out that Aya-chan and I had already made love once. Would I end up like that rooster in the temple yard? Just thinking about it was enough to make me shiver with fear. *Listen, bud—why don't you give Ayako's pussy a little rub for me sometime? It's itching for some attention. She keeps going on about "Ikushima-san, Ikushima-san* . . . " I knew he was making it all up, but precisely because he was making it up it sounded so much like Aya-chan's real voice in my ears.

19

Early one evening, I heard someone knocking on my door. It made me vaguely tense. When I said, "come in," a completely unexpected visitor appeared in the doorway. His name was Yamane Yōji. No sooner did he see me than he smiled and said, "Ikushima! I've found you!"

He and I had had some rather involved dealings for a while when I lived in Tokyo.

"How'd you find me?"

"There's ways." I looked at the raw organs in front of me. This was one scene I wouldn't have wanted anyone to see. Here I, too, was, a toad in the bottom of a pipe. I remembered Shimpei's shout. "Can I come on in?"

"Oh, sure."

"It took some searching, you know. I wrote to your mother, but she answered back *I have nothing to do with my son anymore. Actually, I have no idea where he is.* It was a bit of a shock."

"I see. It stands to reason my mother wouldn't know where I am any more. It's been a long time since I've seen her. A couple of years ago when we met, she didn't even bother to ask me what I was doing at the time."

"That was considerate of her."

"No, she's disappointed with me."

"You disappointed me, too, you know, being so shiftless. I couldn't believe it."

In fact I was the kind of feckless individual who would only disappoint everybody, my mother included. I was disappointed in myself. But why had Yamane taken the trouble to come see me? Was I worth the effort? No, it was inconceivable, even to me, that Yamane would just want to pay me a visit. He had a job at some newspaper company, doing background coordination for various sporting events. I always thought he had a distinctly chilly air about him; he never let anybody past a certain distance into his personal space, and he didn't cross that boundary in the other direction toward others. He withdrew quickly if he met pressure, but a moment later he would always be back where he was. If I asked about something that had to do with him, he'd blow me off with "It doesn't really matter, does it?" and never say anything about himself. We did associate after a fashion, but he always stayed just out of reach.

"What brings you here?"

"I came to see how you're making it these days, of course. If it turned out you were dead, I'd want to know how you died."

"I see."

"Well, I'm glad you're all right—though I had no intention of lifting a finger for you if you weren't, you understand."

"No doubt."

"I just came to see what kind of situation you were in. It would have been fine if I had arrived just in time to see you kick the bucket. No harm intended; I just wanted to see everything, that's all."

"As you can see, this is my life—surrounded by the stink of spoiled meat."

"I learned a lot from you, you know. How about a drink?"

"Sure."

Yamane had bought a half-gallon bottle of saké and some snacks at the liquor store nearby. Toward the end of my stay in Tokyo, I had cadged a lot of drinks and money from him, none of which I had ever returned. It became something of an obsession for me, but he never seemed to mind. I was doing it just to get some kind of rise out of him, in fact, but he never obliged. And now here he was, saying he had learned a lot from me.

"Why don't you stop doing that for today?"

"You say 'stop doing that,' but this is my work. I can't very well quit."

Yamane ran his tongue over his lips.

"Somebody's coming to pick it up tomorrow morning, without fail. You have schedules at your office, too, don't you?" I said.

"What do you mean—surely this isn't your real job, is it?"

"This is it. This is what I do for a living."

"So you're planning to keep doing this from now on?"

"You can say what you want, but there are plenty of people in the world who make it their life's work to put meat on skewers so you can sit in a restaurant, drink saké, and eat *yakitori*. Right?"

"No, no, that's not what I'm talking about. This isn't the kind of thing that nobody but you can do. Anybody could do this. Even my married older sister makes *yakitori* on skewers at home."

"Hmm, of course. And your sister's good-looking, and smart to boot."

"Ikushima, listen to me. I'm not putting down *yakitori*. I understand it takes a lot of patience. But it's just not your kind of job."

"All right, but you *were* putting it down, you know. Actually, I don't think much of it myself."

"Then why are you doing such a thing in a place like this?"

"Because I don't have anyplace else to go."

"That's a lie."

"Nope. There's no place left for me but here."

"That can't be. There's something scary inside you, because you've lost all concern for your own welfare. That woman was telling me about you: "He's the kindest man I ever met. He's never violent; he's honest; he's fun to listen to. But when I'm with him, I sometimes get terribly frightened. There are times when I feel like a hen, but I'm not sitting on a hen's eggs; they're a snake's." A woman's intuition can be pretty amazing, don't you think?"

"I guess so. She told me the same thing, actually, but I didn't understand what she was saying. She got disillusioned with me, just like you did."

"She was afraid of you."

"No, it wasn't like that while she and I were together."

"I suppose so. Anybody would have said you were just an ordinary company man in those days. But she already knew, even before you did, that you would be like this one day."

"There's no hope for me. I'm still the way I was back then."

"You pushed yourself off the cliff, just as she suspected you would. She was scared. She said 'Ikushima-san's like this now, but there's no telling what he's going to do.'"

"Maybe so."

When he first found out that I was interested in that woman, Yamane had backed off. There were signs, though, that she was interested in him; it became obvious when he backed away from her. She got nervous; I tried to patch things up in a panic, but it was too late. Yamane asked me to meet him at a restaurant in Fukagawa and told me "I'm getting out." Hearing him say that was hard for me. I had been watching nervously as her obvious feelings for him grew into something serious. If I hadn't taken an interest in her, things would probably have worked out so that she and Yamane got together. Yet after grilling me, he had the gall to say, "So you and she—well, how nice. I see. But now that I understand your feelings, I'm afraid I couldn't have anything to do with that woman." It sounded as though he wanted to say he had touched something unclean.

"Say, don't you want to know how she's doing now?"

I didn't answer.

"Surely there's no way you aren't curious—you were pretty tight with her back then, weren't you?" He stuck his tongue in his cheek and grinned. "She found a dagger hidden in the back of your closet once, you know."

"What? I never had such a thing."

"Don't play dumb, Ikushima my friend. I know you were planning to go after somebody back then."

I was speechless.

"She saw the dagger and the notes where you planned out the attack. She even saw where you wrote out a statement of justification for it. You always did like to do things the old-fashioned way, didn't you?"

Still I said nothing.

"You gave up on the assassination attempt and pushed

yourself off a cliff instead. Now you're about to drive yourself to the very brink of existence. If not, why would you be so serious about a job that even you say is absurd? The woman at the Igaya was talking about it, too."

"What? You went and saw the old bag?"

"Of course. She said she'd never seen anybody who went about a job like this as intently as you do. By the way, what'd you do with the dagger?"

Still silent.

"Ikushima-san, isn't there some kind of work only you can do? How about it?"

I knew what kind of work he was talking about, of course, but I answered, "No, not for me, now. I'm just a stray bullet. I've abandoned the world."

"That's not true."

"You can say what you want, but nowadays I—"

"Why are you being so childish?"

"The way it is, is fine with me."

"Do you seriously feel that way?"

"Yep. I'm happy with it."

"Happy? Try saying that again."

"I've given up on myself already, Yamane-san."

This time it was his turn to be silent.

"I have nothing left to throw away. All there is now is—"

"Look me in the eye while you're talking, would you?"

I glared back at him.

"Are you still writing fiction?"

"Fiction? I never wrote fiction."

Yamane made an impatient noise between his teeth. "There's no other way of life left for you except to write. Aren't there some things that people can only come to grips with by writing? Of course, writing fiction's sort of like scooping the moon's reflection out of a pond with a basket, I suppose."

"It's crap."

"Tch. I can see I've wasted my time coming here. If you're not going to keep writing, you and I are through."

I first met this man after I sent a novel called *Preparations for a Country Funeral* to a magazine and—to my surprise—it got published. Masako introduced him to me as her friend. He was as much a straight arrow as I was.

At the time, the wage-slave life had me terribly depressed. Groping around for something that would revitalize my spirit, I wandered into an antique shop in a city on the northern coast and found a dagger. They told me a young widow had sold it, saying she had never known that her deceased husband had owned such a thing. It was signed by a famous seventeenth-century swordsmith and had a deep gash on one side of the blade; I could see my sad-eyed, haggard features reflected in its polished steel. I brought it back to Tokyo and put it away in my closet. That was all. But I thought I could sense the soul of its previous owner still inside it, silently watching. Moved by that image, I had dashed off the novel at a ferocious pace.

While I was out buying sushi at a nearby shop, Seiko Nēsan came by. She was sitting down with Yamane when I returned, which immediately made me uneasy. She had brought sashimi and some skewers of grilled meat that I had cut up.

"I'm having a hard time here, honey. This guy's asking a lot of questions about you," she said.

"I'm just trying to find out a little about what you do every day, that's all." He had already finished about half the bottle of saké and was sounding a little drunk.

"He's grilling me like some kind of cop. Who is he?"

"He's a buddy from my days back in Tokyo."

"Oh, yeah; he said that when he first came by, but where's he get off giving somebody the third degree?"

"Yamane-san: what time is it?" I asked.

"About four minutes to nine."

It was the busiest time of night for the Igaya, and I was dropping a hint for Seiko Nēsan's benefit. But she showed no inclination to go, even though she'd been ready enough to leave the time she came by after my face got cut. I put down the sushi and three cold beers I'd bought. Once the three of us had each downed a beer, Seiko Nēsan spoke up: "You know, your buddy gives me the creeps."

"What?"

"He may be your good buddy and all that, but you know, he asks me 'why is he living in a place like this?' I told him when he first showed up: it makes no difference to me why."

"Well, I beg your pardon, ma'am." A fleck of beer foam flew out of Yamane's mouth.

"Yamane-san—that's your name, right?—You ought to be ashamed of yourself, talking like that. What do you mean, 'a place like this'?"

"Oh, my. I'm terribly sorry."

The windows and the hall door were wide open, but the stifling heat stayed trapped in the apartment.

"Ikushima-han, you said a minute ago that this guy was a buddy of yours from back in Tokyo. I guess that means you're his kind, too."

"Well, yes, I did associate with him during my days in Tokyo. If he let slip his true feelings, then those feelings are mine, too, and I apologize. But—"

"But, what? I'd like to know, too, actually, what you're doing 'in a place like this.' Everybody does, you know; they wonder why you're just rotting away here."

"That's right, Ikushima—"

"And you—you've got some nerve cutting in like that," she said. Yamane pursed his lips.

"No, Seiko Nēsan, I'm glad I came here. It's not a lie. If he really meant what he said at your place, then I really mean what I say, too. It's the truth, just the same."

"Really?"

"Yes."

"Listen: you people are intellectuals. You've got a way with words. Somebody like me, you can pull the wool over their eyes like taking candy from a baby. But you haven't answered the question, why you're rotting in a place like this."

"Yeah, Ikushima-san, how about it?"

"You, hush! You're an outsider, aren't you?"

Some more beer foam escaped Yamane's lips.

"No, I'm a fall guy—a loser," I said.

"I think you know this good and well already, Ikushima-han, but you're not going to make it around here with an attitude like that. You know that woman that comes around here mumbling those weird Buddhist chants?"

"Yes—"

"You say you're a loser, you say you're no good, but there's a difference in what people say and the way they really are. She's not reciting those prayers just for the hell of it. Those men that pay good money to get in her pants aren't just fooling around, either."

There was a spell of silence. I was sure Yamane had no clue about the chants. A white moth was fluttering around the hanging electric light.

"You can call yourself a loser and a fall guy and all that, Ikushima-han, but that's just intellectual crap. It only sounds like it makes sense. That woman's chanting doesn't make any sense, either; it's just gobbledygook, but you know, she's hurting like hell inside the whole time she's doing it."

"That's right, Ikushima. You need to give it some serious thought."

"You! That's just the kind of intellectual crap I'm talking about!"

"Oh—Ha, ha, well, OK, OK." The drink was really going to Yamane's head now.

"Ikushima-han, this man's like a saint. He went to a lot of trouble to hunt you down in a place like this. I don't need to know why you decided to come here and just rot; I don't care. But you know, I've put myself in your hands."

"Oh, no, I—"

"You didn't think twice about saying you'd go to that phone booth at the train station for me, did you—just like that?"

I didn't say anything.

"That's the real you. There's no 'fall guy' about it."

"But, that time—"

"Right. Right. OK, OK." Yamane chimed in again.

"This man's so funny, Ikushima-han. You know what he did? He comes into my joint and stands there like a statue, and asks me 'What does 'living' mean?'" I told him damn if I know about anything that complicated."

"Ah, yes; you—the owner of the Igaya. What does 'living' mean? OK! OK!" Yamane was definitely under the influence.

"Think about it yourself, Mister. Damn intellectuals, they don't have a lick of sense." Seiko Nēsan was beginning to sound seriously angry. "They talk about Karl Marx said this, and Fukuzawa Yukichi said that, and they know a lot about what other people said; they come into my place and go on about stuff like that all the time. That's just intellectual bullshit."

"This is great! OK! OK!"

The steamy night air drifting up from the dead-still waters of Osaka Bay was an oppressive presence in the room. The moth was still fluttering around persistently under the shade on the light bulb.

"To tell the truth, Seiko Nēsan, I really don't know why I'm here."

"Huh?"

"I just ended up here, like a loose pair of pants sliding down."

"See, I thought so. Knowing you, I figured you'd say something like that sooner or later. I don't know why I stay around here, either," she said.

"Really?"

"Of course, silly. Is there anybody in this world that does?"

"OK! OK!" Yamane again.

"Hush. You're such a—"

"Ah, ha, ha!"

"This man here's sure pleased with himself since he found you, Ikushima-han."

"Oh, no. I came here from Tokyo because I was pissed off."

"You fathead," she said.

Yamane went on: "Really, Miss Proprietress of the Igaya, you ought to quit worrying about this guy and think a little more about yourself."

"Me? It doesn't make any difference what happens with me."

"Surely you don't mean that, lady."

"No, I—"

"Come on, Seiko Nēsan."

"Well, I'm going back to the shop. Didn't mean to hang around so long."

Yamane was eating grilled tripe from some pig that had died from disease. I was eating it, too; it was the first time I had ever eaten any of it, but Yamane didn't know that. As long as he was eating some, though, I couldn't avoid it.

I wondered what Seiko Nēsan was thinking when she cooked and brought this stuff. In my mind I pictured her lonely looking back as she hurried through the dark streets after she left. She talked tough, but she was after all an aging woman no one took an interest in any more. The little zelkova bonsai she'd brought here testified to that. But it was better not to get too involved with her; she'd lived a hard life, alone. She said Yamane was "like a saint." Indeed, he spent nearly four years looking before he found me. I couldn't possibly imagine being worth that, but there was something significant about Yamane's coming here.

20

The zelkova bonsai that Seiko Nēsan had brought me was starting to die. No amount of water was going to keep it alive without sunshine all day long in this hot apartment. Still, there was something in me that was determined not to let it die. I set it out in the empty lot behind the building every night, hoping the night dew and morning sun would help, and took it back in each morning after Sai-chan left. But this living thing had gone into a fatal decline, and it gradually continued to wither.

God and the devil coexist in every human being. Naturally, Yamane Yōji was no exception. Yamane's visit made me think. He was the kind of man who, after taking the trouble to get a job at the newspaper, didn't even try for a position on the editorial staff where all the glamour was; instead, he opted for a background job in event coordination. He chose to stay in the shadows and calmly watch as the others struggled in the light. And that was his point of view when he came to see what had become of me. It was just like him, again, when I asked him how he was doing now, to answer, "Oh, it doesn't really matter, does it?" and say not a word about himself. There was one difference, however: he had not really come just to check on my present circumstances.

Yamane had come to tell me to "scoop the moon out of the pond in a basket." There was really nothing more to it. He wouldn't lose his life saying that, and the words were hardly going to make a deep impression on me. What Aya-chan said that night—"Stand up"; "Unhook me"; "Ah . . . "; "Do it"—she uttered those words at a point where her life could have been hanging in the balance. I suppose Yamane meant to say I ought to write something that might cost me my life, but he wasn't about to put his own life on the line with his words. His words were just empty talk, whereas Aya-chan's originated from the very core of her being; the shock of those words had left a deep, penetrating wound in my existence.

As these thoughts went through my mind, I grew impatient with Yamane. His urging me to write provoked me to resistance: *why the hell should I?* It was really just an obsession of his. Writing fiction wasn't anything exalted; what difference is there between that and fooling with the guts of diseased pigs and cattle? The two of us had loved the same woman, and both of us had lost her. I suspected it was the very intensity of this sense of loss that had driven him to search and find me four years later.

The apartment across the hall was silent. That reddish-haired woman no longer came. I hadn't seen Horimayu-san since that day earlier in the month when he yelled at me. I hadn't heard Shimpei's voice downstairs for a while; there was no sign of Aya-chan, either. It was a holiday afternoon in mid-August, during the O-Bon Festival when people go home to visit family and their ancestors' graves; sprawling in my hot, darkened apartment, I felt almost as if I would suffocate. I had no desire to go anywhere. A fly circled lazily around the room.

As I was working that hot afternoon, Seiko Nēsan came by, wearing a simple dress unbuttoned partway down the front. She seemed agitated. I hadn't seen her since that night Yamane came to visit.

"Thanks for the other night," I said to her.

"Oh, never mind. I was glad he came so I could find out more about you."

The old woman was always saying things that stung. Rummaging in her bag for a lighter with one hand, holding the cigarette in the other, she suddenly looked at me.

"By the way, aren't you keeping something for Mayu-san?"

"Uh—what?" I immediately thought about the box, but in the next instant I blurted out: "Well, no, actually."

I knew, however, that my face had betrayed surprise. She looked at me steadily for a while.

"Ikushima-han, I've told you this already, but I'll say it again. Mayu-san's a dangerous man. Remember that and watch what you do."

"Yes, ma'am."

I wondered if she had missed the change in my expression. I decided that she had chosen to ignore it, but I couldn't very well contradict myself now. Having the box in my possession was a continuing source of anxiety, it was true; as Seiko Nēsan said, I too was aware how dangerous a man Horimayu-san was. It made me feel all the more like confessing to her I had it, but I was caught in a dilemma: the very fact that I knew how dangerous he was made me afraid to let her know. She sat there smoking, with a harsh look in her eyes. My undershirt was soaked already; the air in the room was so steamy and hot that it actually felt hard to breathe. Sweat was trickling down Seiko Nēsan's temples. I gathered up the courage and decided to ask some questions.

"I used to hear Shimpei downstairs sometimes, but I haven't heard anything at all lately."

"That so?"

"And I haven't noticed Mayu-san coming upstairs in a while, either. I used to see him and Shimpei now and then, until just a while ago."

"The boy's gone. Sent away to a foster home in Gojō, Nara Prefecture."

"He—what?"

"You might say they got rid of him. But you know, he's better off there than he was here."

"I see." I recalled the sadness in Shimpei's eyes when he made his confession to me about ruining his precious origami toys, Mr. Rabbit and Mr. Crocodile.

"It sure is hot in this apartment."

"Yes, it is."

"I don't know how you stand it in here. It's hot as hell. I can hardly breathe." Seiko Nēsan opened her mouth, revealing the silver caps on her back teeth.

"I don't have anywhere else to go, after all."

"What the hell you talking about? Didn't that guy—what's his name, Yamane?—didn't he come by the other day?"

"Yes, he did. But he just came to see what kind of situation I was in these days. He said he didn't have any interest in helping me and left. He told me if I wanted to get back up again, I should pick myself up."

"Then why don't you?"

"But I—"

"Still got the hots for Aya-chan?"

"I beg your pardon?"

"What kind of voice is that? A big man like you, you sound like you're drooling at the mouth. It's a damn shame."

"No, I really don't—"

"Well, never mind, that's all right, let your rotten balls sing a song. By the way, starting tomorrow Sai-chan's not going to be coming by for a while."

"Which means—?"

Seiko Nēsan stubbed out her cigarette. "That's all." She took a brown envelope out of her handbag and put it down on the tatami floor. It was the kind she always put my pay in.

"Here's for the month up to yesterday. Sai-chan's not coming by anymore."

"Oh."

She looked me directly in the eyes. Her back teeth clenched, she seemed to be holding back some kind of anger. No doubt Yamane's visit had driven her to this decision. "You got someplace to go?"

"Not really."

"I see. Well, I know this is pretty sudden, but I don't want you living here anymore. To put it in plain words, I want you out."

I was speechless.

"You're not the kind that belongs around here. You won't make it."

She stood up and opened the refrigerator door. Aya-chan's panties, wrapped in that day's newspaper, were still in the vegetable drawer at the bottom.

"There's still quite a bit of meat in here. Sorry to ask, but I need you to finish working this up and bring it over, tomorrow or the day after."

"Certainly."

"When you come by, there's something I want to give you. For sure."

I thought I would give her the sachet then, too, and wondered what Seiko Nēsan had in mind to give me. As she put her hand on the doorpost to slip on her clogs, she turned around toward me.

"Oh, by the way—seen Aya-chan around lately?"

"No, not for these past two or three days—"

"Yeah? Listen, do me a favor. If you see her, tell her to get in touch with me as soon as she can. Or just phone me and tell me where and when you saw her."

"I'll do it."

She looked me in the eyes and swallowed hard. "This is for real, you understand?"

"Has something happened?"

"That's none of your business. Just make sure you do it."

Seiko Nēsan left. There was an ominous feeling about the moment as she swallowed hard and looked at me.

I sat motionless in the room for a while, then went downstairs and looked down the dimly lit first-floor corridor. There was no activity in front of the apartment at the end, no sign at all of anyone inside. Actually I hadn't heard any noise from downstairs in the past several days, nor seen Horimayu-san or Aya-chan. I wondered when Shimpei had been taken to Gojō. I realized it was dumb of me, but I didn't even remember the last time I'd seen him. Something was definitely wrong.

Going back to my apartment, I opened the refrigerator door to assure myself the newspaper bundle was still there. I took Horimayu-san's little box out of the closet. Whatever was inside had a solid heft to it. At that moment, someone jerked open the front door.

"Hey, is Miss Kishida around?"

It was Sōda, the one who always had his hand in his pocket. His voice was strained.

"She left a little while ago, actually."

"Where'd she say she was going?"

"She didn't say. I suppose back to her shop."

As he hurried back down the stairs, the sound of his footsteps gave me a sense of urgency. I felt as if I had to do something—but what? I was sure something was going on at that very moment, but couldn't see what it had to do with me. All I sensed were signs and sounds of things going on someplace completely unconnected with me. Still I felt the tension of being dragged little by little into what was already happening.

Eventually night came; the heat in the apartment grew even more oppressive. There was no sound downstairs. I wondered what I was going to do. Once I finished working up the last of the meat, tomorrow or the day after, I would finally have to leave Ama. Yamane's visit was the proximate cause, but in fact I was already a piece of flotsam. I knew Seiko Nēsan wasn't evicting me out of malice; she was just telling me to go back where I belonged. But I no longer had the contacts or relationships I needed for that. First off, nobody would stand security for me, whether I looked for someplace to live or for another job. I was a drifter. About the only kind of job I could get without a security pledge would be in a *pachinko* pinball parlor or someplace peddling counterfeit merchandise. In any case, it wouldn't be honest work. Even Yamane had only come to see what kind of fix I was in; it was turning out now just as he said.

21

The next morning, Sai-chan really did fail to show. Concrete reality hits people in the face with events like this. If I worked at it, I could finish up all the meat in the refrigerator that day. I undid the newspaper wrapping and looked at Aya-chan's panties. Feeling a stab of pain, I hurriedly put them away and got to work on the meat. I told myself that I should try to work at the same pace as always, but what next?—nothing left but to pack up my things and leave.

When I got back from eating lunch, a stranger was standing outside my door. By his looks, he was a young *kusubori*— a cheap gangster. He went downstairs as soon as he saw me. As I went inside, there were footsteps on the stairs, and then Horimayu-san was at the door. The young gangster seemed to be back, too, standing outside in the hall. Horimayu-san came in without asking.

"Thanks for your patience, my friend. How about getting out the box I asked you to keep for me?"

"Oh, that? Sure."

I was relieved at the thought of being able to return the box directly to Horimayu-san, as I had been thinking about leaving

it with Seiko Nēsan when I left town. I got it out immediately
and offered it to him, but he didn't reach for it.

"Listen, I need you to do me another favor. You game?"

"What is it?" Suddenly I felt very uneasy.

"It's no big deal. I just need you take this box to Daimotsu
for me."

"Who, me?"

"Yeah. I hate to ask you to go in this heat, but—" He pulled
a scrap of paper out of his breast pocket. "Here's where I want
you to go." The scrap of paper was a map. "Here's Daimotsu
Station. Here's where you're going. The first floor of this building's a vegetable shop. Go down the narrow alley here to the
side. There's a door to your left, and inside's a stairway going
up. There's a man named Saitō waiting on the third floor. He's
the one I want you to deliver the box to."

I said nothing.

"Don't worry; it's all worked out. All you have to do is give it
to him."

"Uh—"

"Saitō's about forty, with a mole right here. And here—this
is train fare."

He put a ten-thousand-yen note in my hand, turned around,
and walked out, leaving me alone. I felt myself being sucked
deeper and deeper into uncertainty. I wondered if it wouldn't be
too late to go tell Seiko Nēsan the truth, but the opportunity was
gone. That young gangster type would probably be keeping an
eye on me from now on; there would be no escape. The flood of
evil that had been pent up in secret was beginning to overflow.

From Deyashiki, Daimotsu Station was two stops toward
Osaka on the Hanshin line. Standing in front of the station,
I could see a *pachinko* parlor and next door a shop selling

Buddhist religious goods. I turned down a side street and after a little while came to a three-story building with a vegetable shop on the first floor, just like on the map. The third floor had a row of blank windows facing the glaring sun, all with closed blinds; an air-conditioning unit stuck out from one of them. I considered walking past at first, but changed my mind after realizing that somebody might be watching me; I turned down the alley. It would be dangerous to hesitate. I put my hand on the doorknob. Inside, the stairs were right in front of me. It was very quiet.

My clogs rattled on the stairs as I walked up. There was a locked, steel-clad door closing off the second floor. The third floor was the same; there was no identification on the door. I took a deep breath and knocked. I waited, then knocked again; this time, somebody called out abruptly from inside: "Who's there?"

"I'm here on an errand for Horimayu-san."

There was a rattle as the door was unlocked, and a fortyish man peered out. His face reminded me of a lobster's head. "Come on in."

The interior was an office. The door shut and locked behind me; the sound shook me to the core. I stepped forward. At the back of the room were a desk, some lockers with a small Shinto altar on a shelf above, and a large framed picture on the wall. The most impressive feature of the office, however, was the lavish suite of reception furniture in the middle of the room. On the sofa in front of the coffee table sat another man, rather younger. He had what we call "three-white eyes"—a condition where the white shows on three sides of his iris instead of just two. Lobsterhead sat down beside him and said to me, "Have a seat." He had a mole at the base of his left eyebrow. Three-

Whites was polishing a pair of white shoes. I sat down on the sofa but couldn't sit back and relax; I was sure it gave them the impression I didn't have much nerve. Three-Whites's eyebrows were shaved; he had something that looked like a rosary wrapped around his right wrist.

I took the wrapped box out of my bag and laid it on the table. Three-whites put his shoes down, reached out, unwrapped the box, and took off the lid. Inside was something wrapped in a newspaper advertising insert. When the paper was peeled away, a black pistol appeared. Three-Whites picked it up, examined it closely, and pulled out the magazine. It was loaded. Lobsterhead kept his eyes on me the whole time. Three-Whites pushed the pistol over to Lobsterhead and said, "This is it. This is the rod, all right." He had a Tokyo accent.

"That so?" was Lobsterhead's only response. He still hadn't taken his eyes off me. My errand was done; I wanted to get up, but his stare held me immobile.

"You like to help people out, don't you?" Lobsterhead said.

"I suppose so." Still, I didn't understand how this could be, considering I had only accepted this task at Horimayu-san's behest. I wondered if Lobsterhead might be making some kind of mistake, but in any case his speaking to me created a break.

"Well, I'd better go," I said, then stood up and immediately turned my back on them. I heard some kind of noise behind me, but I kept walking toward the door. I had a sensation of something cold rushing down my back. I unhooked the chain on the door, turned the handle, and pushed; the landing appeared. My hand slipped off the door handle as I stepped out. The door slammed shut with an unexpectedly loud noise; the vibration shook me to the heart. I walked slowly down the stairs, and with each step all the hair on my body seemed to stand on end.

The fierce summer sun hit me in the face as I stepped outside. My throat was parched. I started walking in a direction
away from the train station. I wanted to walk back home, to
settle my mind. After I had gone some distance, a white car
pulled up alongside; it gave me a shock. The window slid down,
and the guy who had come with Horimayu-san the other day
peered out at me. Another man was driving.

"How'd it go?" he asked.

"I handed it over."

"You made sure it was Saitō, didn't you?"

The question unnerved me; I groped for words. "There was
a man with a mole right here, and one other."

"Good. Did they say anything?"

"No, nothing—"

Actually, Three-Whites had said, "This is it," after looking
the pistol over closely. Anyway, the man in the car ordered the
driver to go on. As the car sped off, I could feel all the strength
draining away from my body.

It was almost dark when I got back to Deyashiki. I had stopped
on the way at a cheap restaurant to drink a beer. I thought about
dropping in at Horimayu-san's to report but decided I didn't
have the stomach for it and went on upstairs. As usual, the dark
apartment smelled of meat when I walked in the door. The heat
was intense, almost palpable. When I turned on the light, I saw
a piece of paper on the cutting board, with writing on it:

> Come to the platform at tennōji Station on the Osaka loop
> line tomorrow. at noon, or if you can't make it then, 7 pm.
> Ayako

Tennōji is a suburb south of Osaka. I swallowed hard, feeling suddenly chilled. I stuffed the piece of paper in my pocket.

There was an icy sensation in back of my eyes. Today was August 18. I took the paper back out, read it over several more times, and stuck it back in my pocket. My chest was heaving. Intense memories flooded back of that night when Aya-chan came upstairs. I listened out but heard nothing. I wondered if Horimayu-san was in his apartment downstairs. What did he do after coming by my place? I knew the other one had tailed me after that. I straightened up the chunks of meat and left the apartment about a half hour after they did, so Aya-chan must have come after that. Seiko Nēsan had asked me yesterday to tell her when I saw Aya-chan; it must mean that Aya-chan had been missing for several days. Was Horimayu-san down there now? If Aya-chan's relationship with him had taken an ominous turn, it must have been a considerable risk for her to come up to my apartment. I wondered again about telling Seiko Nēsan, but I knew that was impossible. One slip and the word would be out about Aya-chan and me; that would be the end of everything.

I went downstairs and looked down the hall toward Horimayu-san's apartment. No sign of activity. I went outside, but his apartment was on the side away from the street. The lights were off in the apartment where Aya-chan and Shimpei had been living.

I went back upstairs. Taking out the paper again, I put it in the ashtray and set it on fire. After it was nothing but ashes, I turned out the light. The intense heat clung to me all over. The ashes glowed faintly red for a while, then died out. Thoughts of Aya-chan's visit that night continued to play in my head. Something was definitely behind the unsettled events that followed Seiko Nēsan's visit yesterday. Again I wondered if Horimayu-san was downstairs. I wondered what would happen if I went to Tennōji tomorrow. I was certain to be drawn irreversibly into a whirlpool of evil; it was certain to be fatal. I clenched my back teeth, feeling the kind of dread that comes as an erection begins to fail. Now was the time to run, if I was going to, but I couldn't do something like that. After I delivered the last of the skewered meat to Seiko Nēsan tomorrow, I would have nowhere to go.

I turned the light back on, took the last of the meat out of the refrigerator, and went to work.

22

The next morning, a man's voice jolted me out of a sound sleep.

"Ayako! Ayako! It's me! Open up!"

He was pounding violently on the door across the hall in a state of extreme distress; his voice was bloodcurdling. I kept still and listened. He soon quit and ran noisily down the stairs. I could sense his desperation; I was sure it was the man who had left word with me for Aya-chan that time, saying he was her brother.

I couldn't stand it any longer. I had finished the skewers last night; I had intended to drop them off at the Igaya on the way to Tennōji Station so that I would get there before noon, but after hearing him I was suddenly afraid to go see Seiko Nēsan. I starting preparing to leave immediately, bundling up my underwear and other bare necessities in a *furoshiki* cloth. I decided to leave behind the winter things, like the coat I was wearing when I first came to town.

Finally, I opened the refrigerator door; the skewers were stacked in neat rows. I figured Seiko Nēsan would find them eventually. I took out Aya-chan's panties, still wrapped in the newspaper; I put them in my carrying bag and shut the door. It was painful, though, not to leave some parting word for Seiko Nēsan. I opened the refrigerator again. Sticking my head inside, I soundlessly formed the words *Sorry, Seiko Nēsan. Thanks for everything.* I closed the door once more, as if sealing the words inside, and hurried out of the building.

It was 9:12 a.m. when I got to Deyashiki Station. The clock was the one I had watched so impatiently once before, but I couldn't remember for sure anymore when that had been. This kind of thing didn't matter anymore, however. There was no telling who might be spying on me; I couldn't stay here any longer. When I asked the man at the ticket gate what time the next train was due, he responded with a leisurely question of his own: "Eastbound or west?"

Just then the station bell signaled the arrival of a westbound train for Kobe. I decided to get on it. It was going in the opposite direction, but I would be able to change at Nishinomiya to an eastbound express and get to Osaka without any more stops. All the strength drained away from me after I got on the train. The car was packed with fans going to the national high school baseball championship games at Kōshien Stadium, near Nishinomiya. Aya-chan's brother's voice was still echoing in my ears.

The train traveled away from Ama with every station it passed, but at the same time it was taking me away from Osaka, where Aya-chan was waiting. Little by little, I began to relax and notice the scenery outside the train windows. A little girl, crying and screaming, was running after a woman pedaling off on a bicycle; then she stopped, and the scene went out of view.

When the train stopped at Kōshien Station, I could hear the crowd cheering in the stadium. A lot of passengers got off, and the car suddenly looked empty. The train started moving again. Why had I run away from Ama? I could have gone on and delivered the skewered meats to Seiko Nēsan as if I knew nothing, exchanged a few polite words, come back to my apartment to pick things up—I could figure it out that far, but I hadn't a clue what I would have done after that.

Of course, I could still change my mind and not go to Tennōji. I could go to Kyoto and drop in on Harada-san and throw away my chance—but I really couldn't do that. Aya-chan had come upstairs to me that night in secret. Throwing away the chance would be throwing my own life away. Hadn't I been doing that all my life, over and over? Hadn't I just now thrown away the chance to say a proper goodbye to Seiko Nēsan?

The train pulled into Nishinomiya Station, but I didn't get up from my seat; I couldn't. I could ride all the way to Motomachi Station in Kobe, the end of the line, and still switch to an express. The train started off again. It was a local that stopped at every station. I was afraid of going to Tennōji; station by station, the train was taking me farther and farther away.

At Ashiya Station, I had a sudden impulse and got off the train along with a group of other passengers. While the rest walked quite naturally toward the exit gates, I stood there as if frozen and stared up at the clock. It was still before ten; I could make it to Tennōji in an hour. But instead of crossing over to the other platform, I walked out of the station.

The station was built over the Ashiya River. Both sides of the river were lined with quiet neighborhoods, with finer houses than any I'd ever known. As I walked along the road beside the river looking at these neighborhoods, I was suddenly reminded of the recurring nightmares I used to have back in Tokyo: of running around with my back on fire. A refined-looking lady walked past me with a fluffy white dog on a leash. The thought suddenly ran through my mind that life in places like this would be hell. I was vaguely irritated. What did my dreams mean?

Maybe it was fear of falling into a "middle-class lifestyle" if I stayed put. My colleagues in the company had all been infatuated with the middle-class lifestyle. For what? A pseudo-western life, a cyclamen on top of the piano, a fluffy white dog, golf, tennis, western food, music, a car—it was enough to make my skin crawl. That kind of life was the pits; the middle-class lifestyle was utterly distasteful to me. While I lived and worked in Tokyo, the distaste lurked somewhere submerged in my unconscious. Six years of drifting had gradually washed the distaste to the surface, but something else came to the surface at the same time: the realization that I, too, once aspired to the very lifestyle that I now observed with disdain on both banks of the Ashiya River. My feelings toward Masako had been similar. I was infatuated with her, but the infatuation also made me feel something fundamentally unforgivable about myself. This was my original sin, the source of all my guilt.

I reached the sea, the waters of Osaka Bay in midsummer. Reflected sunlight glared off its surface. The evening after I saw this same light on the sea at the mouth of the Yodo River was when Aya-chan suddenly came upstairs. Her words— "Stand up," "Unhook me," "Ah . . . ," "Do it"—came rushing back in my memory over the sound of the waves. The words were spoken in the dark. Still, they were also words, words like those I unexpectedly read one day at the Nakanoshima Library in Osaka:

> . . . *Please pick it up for me.*
> *It's drifting on the waves.*

See, look:
It's just within reach.
I know you've tried to reach out to it
As hard as you could.
The ocean's waters are so angry today;
The waves are trying to swallow even you.
But please don't be afraid,
And get that hat for me . . .

The glittering waves in the bay on the other side of the sun-baked breakwater kept coming into view only to disappear, over and over.

I got on the loop line train at the National Railways' Osaka Station a little after six thirty that evening. It was rush hour; I was riding in a packed car, holding the big cloth bundle in my right hand and my navy blue travel bag in the left. A pocket inside the travel bag held a passbook with the money I had built up at the postal savings bank in the last two years or so, not quite a hundred thousand yen. The only cash on me was the little bit in my pocket that Seiko Nēsan had handed me the day before yesterday. There was probably enough to last me three weeks at most, including lodging at some flophouse. The bag also contained a couple of notebooks, a fountain pen, a bottle of ink, tissues, and a cheap ready made personal seal, the kind all Japanese use for signing documents. That was the sum total of my worldly goods. The flotsam, caught for a while against a post in the water, was adrift once again. I didn't have an insurance card,or a company ID like the one I had when I was working, so this cheap seal I'd bought when I opened the savings account was the only thing now that could identify me. The address on my account was also the one from back in

Nishinomiya. I hadn't had a bath in several days; the stubble on my face grated against the back of my hand.

Going on to Tennōji would be senseless, an act of folly. I was forever being assailed by the cowardice within me. At noon, I had still been sitting on a rock shaded by the pine trees on Ashiya Beach as if I'd lost my senses. The glare from the sea was burning my forearms and the backs of my hands. In the final analysis, there was nowhere else for me to go except Tennōji Station.

The train pulled in to the platform at Tennōji. The face of that little girl chasing the woman on the bicycle this afternoon came back to mind. It was a big station. There were separate platforms for the railway line's outer and inner loops, facing each other. It was quitting time, and an awesome mass of humanity was flowing through the station. I wondered if I would be able to find Aya-chan in this throng. I looked at the station clock: it was still a little before seven.

I was standing where I got off the train. If either of us moved, we might miss each other. The passing of time was stifling. Startled, I suddenly caught sight of Aya-chan on the facing platform; the "barefooted woman" was wearing a white top and white skirt. She was walking along hurriedly, searching for me in the opposite direction. Like it or not, a whole new flow of time was going to begin once she transfixed me with her intense look. I could see her back as she walked farther away. Following her with my eyes, I began walking along the platform on my side; no—as I followed her with my eyes, my feet started to move of their own accord. She turned around; I stopped; our eyes met. A shade of emotion crossed her face; her expression hardened. She smiled for a second, but then the hardness returned to her face as she pointed a finger at me. A train came into the platform on her side, and I thought I saw her running down the stairs; I had only a few seconds left if I wanted to escape. I just stood there.

Aya-chan was coming closer. Slowly but steadily, some emaciated kind of creature was walking toward me with its eyes fixed on mine—no; what approached me was wearing all over it the striking, dark expression that appeared on Aya-chan's face whenever she closed her eyes. It was evening, quitting time; everyone who went by looked exhausted. Aya-chan's cold and alienated expression stood out alone amid the surrounding tumult. Then she smiled, with slightly pursed lips.

"Sorry," she said.

"Oh, it's all right—"

As she started walking, she said, "I couldn't get here at noon today."

"Oh? . . . "

"Were you here?"

"Actually, no."

"Oh, so you couldn't make it either. I was worried because I thought I stood you up. I got here at two and looked all over for you. I even went outside the station for a little bit, I was so nervous."

"I'm really sorry I was late."

"Don't you have to meet Sai-chan every evening when he comes?"

"No. He's not coming anymore."

"Why not?"

"I'll explain later."

We went out through the fare gates. Aya-chan was carrying a sizable fabric handbag. I was awkward looking in my wooden geta clogs, the big cloth-wrapped bundle dangling in one hand.

The two of us wandered around, searching for the station exit. The cloth bundle bounced heavily and clumsily against our legs, but I couldn't very well abandon it; in it were my minimum needs of daily life for the time being. I shoved the bundle into a coin-operated locker in the station. As I looked up after turning the key in the lock, Aya-chan spoke to me.

"I want you to run away with me. Take me with you."

"What?"

She was biting her lower lip as she looked at me.

"Where?"

"Somewhere outside of this world."

I gulped. I had "touched it." I didn't take my eyes off her. She had pretty much guessed the situation from the bundle in my hand. I opened my mouth, but no words came. She turned her back on me and started walking; her back seemed to be declaring some terrible refusal. My legs wouldn't move. She was putting more and more distance between us. It felt as if my inner being were leaking away. I trotted to catch up to her.

Aya-chan was walking silently, looking straight ahead. I had never gotten off at Tennōji Station before. The lively streets were bright with garish neon lights; I had no idea where we were going. I was sure she had been pursued to a point where she had no choice but to try escaping from "this world." The neon lights lit up her back, one color after another, as she walked silently on. The sensation of warm blood surged up from my feet like steam. We turned into a somewhat darker side street.

After going on a little farther, Aya-chan stopped and went into a restaurant. I followed her in. The space was narrow but went back a considerable distance. She sat down at a table for two, facing the back; I walked around and sat across from her.

A waiter came up. Aya-chan ordered fried shrimp and grilled eel liver. He was astute enough to ask, "Two orders each?" and I answered, "Yes, thanks," while watching for her reaction. I sat frozen in my seat, writhing inwardly.

She asked in a subdued voice, "Got any money?"

"Yes. Not much, but I can pick up the tab."

"I need ten million yen."

"I beg your pardon?"

"Well, five million might be enough."

I was at a loss for words.

"If I can't come up with the money, my brother's going to end up in the bay off Daimotsu in a barrel of concrete—you know, an oil drum."

The waiter came back just then with our beer, and Aya-chan went quiet. I recalled Sanada's voice from that morning.

"My brother took his gang's protection-racket money and put it on the horses—in a betting bank." An open beer bottle and two empty glasses stood on the table. "But he got burned. Bad."

"What's a betting bank?"

"It's a deal where you've got a 90 percent chance of making money. But you make only a hundred-ten, a hundred-twenty maybe, on a hundred-yen bet. Of course nobody wants to win just ten or twenty yen, so they don't go in with just one or two thousand at a time. Try putting up a million; now you're talking about a 90 percent chance of making a hundred or two hundred thousand. I heard my brother started out with two million yen."

"But . . ."

"Right. A sure thing went bad. So he threw more money at

it, again and again, trying to make it back. Before he knew it, he was down ten million. Once you start losing, it just makes you nuts and you can't quit."

"I see—" I could feel my vitality seeping away; I was sure Sanada had felt the same. "How about Horimayu-san?"

"He doesn't give a damn, of course. He's like a dead egg. The only thing he lives for is rubbing ink into somebody's skin. But once he's made his marks, he's finished with them."

"I see. He has a hard time, doesn't he?"

"Him? A hard time?"

"Being a dead egg and having to live at the same time." I felt some relief at being able to throw Aya-chan's words back at her. I picked up the beer bottle and filled both glasses.

"You got quite a bit of sun, didn't you?" she said. It startled me.

"I guess so. Just today—"

"You ran away from Seiko Nēsan's place, didn't you?"

"No, I was fired."

"Really? I bet it wasn't easy for her to fire you, after worrying about you so much. But she always said she shouldn't have let you stay in a place like that for so long."

"I see . . . "

"It must have been hard on her. Did she say anything to you when you left?"

"Actually, I left without saying good-bye."

"You didn't!"

The dishes started to arrive. I finally took a sip of my beer and picked up the chopsticks. I was beginning to relax a little; I learned the name of the restaurant, Tenkawa.

"It really shook me up when I saw your missive yesterday."

"Missive?"

"Sorry. Note."

"You know a lot of deep stuff, don't you?"

"Maybe, but none of it's any use."

She smiled slyly.

"Seiko Nēsan's going to be disappointed now, you know."

"Yes, I understand. I've lived my life throwing opportunities away."

"You're always using big words, aren't you? I don't understand stuff like that—'throwing opportunities away.'"

"Sorry."

She shook her hair over her shoulder and laughed. I had lost track of how long it had been since I sat over drinks with a woman like this. I was enjoying it, despite the anxieties I had and so much on my mind. I was enjoying it—but Seiko Nēsan had asked me the day before yesterday to tell her as soon as I saw Aya-chan. I wondered if I should tell Aya-chan about that and about going to Daimotsu on that errand for Horimayu-san yesterday, her brother coming by early that morning, about Shimpei—

Aya-chan was telling me about the bank robber she had seen being arrested in the street while she was waiting for me in Tennōji. "The cops took him away. His face looked like a busted beer bottle, like this. The first thing I thought was for him to run while he could."

If her brother truly was in such a fix, I could understand her sympathetic reaction. You could hardly come up with five or ten million yen without robbing a bank or something. Sanada was doomed. What I'd heard this morning was the voice of a man with his back on fire. Seiko Nēsan had probably found out the details before Aya-chan knew. When she came by that night, several days before Yamane's visit, she gave me a hard time about tailing Aya-chan and warned me not to get any closer to her. Seiko Nēsan must have been trying to keep me out of trouble, but here I was in Tennōji. Still, I wondered if there was really a need for the two of us to escape from "this world."

It was past ten thirty that night when Aya-chan and I left Tenkawa. She paid the tab. We were both a little drunk; we had no particular place to go. Walking down a dimly lit street, I stopped in front of a lovers' hotel called the June Bride.

"We going in here?" she asked.

I nodded, and she responded under her breath, "Might as well—we don't have anywhere else."

As soon as we got into our room, we were in each other's arms without even turning off the light. Our tongues couldn't help seeking each other. We fell straight into bed. There was a smell of sweat; my member was erect. The sunshine I had watched on Osaka Bay that afternoon was glaring inside my head.

> . . . *That hat*
> *Was swallowed by a wave*
> *In an instant, as I stumbled.*

Aya-chan suddenly moved her face away; my stubble seemed to be irritating her skin.

She stood up and went to the bathroom. I heard the rush of water. Coming back, she took a pack of cigarettes out of her handbag and lit one. I was thirsty; my chest was still heaving. She stubbed out the cigarette in the ashtray and stood up again. She undid the zipper and hook of her skirt; as it fell to the floor, I was startled to see traces of ink on her skin from her hips down to her buttocks. One foot at a time, she stepped out of her panties. With her back turned to me, she pulled off her white cotton shirt in a single movement. Her entire back was covered by the figure of a phoenix in intense colors, its wings outspread. It was the tattoo I had seen, only dimly, back at the apartment in Deyashiki, when I thought it looked like the pattern on a snake. In front of my eyes now, I could see that it was a beautifully feminine design. I shivered, as though I had goose bumps in my soul. I felt the kind of fear I'd experienced when I saw the tattoo of Fudō on the back of that man at the bathhouse in Deyashiki, maybe even more intense. Seeing those dazzling colors chilled me. A phoenix was rising out of a red lotus blossom with green leaves.

"Unhook me."

After I unhooked her bra, she slipped out of my arms and went into the bathroom. I immediately heard the shower running full blast. As I stripped, too, the smell of sweaty underwear stung my nostrils.

Aya-chan was moving around under the shower, covered in suds, catching the rush of hot water in her face. Her wet hair clung in wisps around her shoulders. I stood still, watching. The torrent of water that had washed the phoenix was running headlong down the drain. That "dead egg" of a man had defiled her body with his spirit. My erection gradually failed. Horimayu-san's words came back to me as an ugly memory: *Listen, bud—why don't you give Ayako's pussy a little rub for me sometime? It's itching for some attention. She's hot for you to do it, not me.*

Aya-chan turned around, looked at me, and came out of the shower. Water was dripping from every part of her body; it was almost dazzling. Her breasts were standing proud; my penis was still limp. When I got into the shower, it felt as though all my sweat-clogged pores were breathing freely again. Aya-chan lathered up my buzz-cut scalp with shampoo, then soaped a towel and scrubbed me from the shoulders down my back, to my anus, and even between my toes. My penis abruptly stiffened as she grasped it and worked it in her fingers.

We made violent love as soon as we both got out of the shower, but our passion didn't approach the heights it had reached that night in Deyashiki. I went flat on my face after only one ejaculation, and she rolled over with her back to me. Maybe it was because I had stopped and obeyed her command to put on the condom that was supplied with the room. I got up and cleaned myself off. There was a fetid smell of semen. When you grab a snake, it tries to get away by releasing a foul-smelling secretion; the odor of semen is just like the smell of that snake's slime. Aya-chan was lying on her stomach, the phoenix's wings spread wide on her back. I looked closer and saw that the phoenix had a human face. The face of a child. It reminded me for a moment of Shimpei, but then I the same bloodshot look in its eyes as in Horimayu-san's. Chinese characters were drawn like flames coming out of its mouth: *unite the self with emptiness; rejoice in eternal purity.*

I leaned over as if to cover the image with my body and touched it with my lips. The phoenix was watching me with pitiless eyes. Every cell in my body shivered; those eyes were the eyes of the "dead egg" man. As I stared at them, Aya-chan spoke with her face still buried in the bed.

"It's called a *kalavinka.*"

"*Kalavinka?*"

"They say it's a bird that lives in paradise. It has a face like a person, body and wings like a bird, and sings with the

Buddha's voice. Mayu told me. There's a picture of it on a postage stamp."

I offered no reply.

I supposed that meant the *kalavinka*'s words were the voice of Buddha. In Greek mythology there are also creatures called sirens with a bird's body and a woman's head. According to legend they, too, sang with a beautiful voice; any man who heard their song was doomed to madness and destruction.

"I grew up on Ragpickers' Row in Ama, you know, living with trash all around. It was creepy getting a lotus flower put on me, but after the ink was rubbed in, at least it finally sank in what kind of woman I was. I grew up eating soup made with dirty water. I don't want anything anymore, except the money to save my brother."

I kept staring at the eyes of the paradise bird. The face was that of a child, but the eyes were cold like those of any bird. I remembered the chicken's eye Horimayu-san put out in the shrine courtyard. And I remembered, too, the meat of the countless chickens I'd cut up.

"So you don't know what a *kalavinka* is?" she asked.

"No, I don't."

"Wow. There's something even you don't know?"

Aya-chan raised herself up and pulled her handbag toward her. She took out a notepad and wrote out the ideograms for *kalavinka* for me: in Japanese, the Sanskrit name is written *ka-ryō-bin-ga*. It wasn't a phoenix, after all. I began to feel a desire for her body again but was hesitant to reach for her.

"Uh . . ."

"What's the matter? Want to do it again?"

"Well . . ."

Aya-chan gave me a long look, then pushed me down onto

the bed. After manipulating my member, she took it in her mouth and began to caress it. She was persistent in her attention. I felt as though I were being caressed by the *kalavinka*'s flaming tongue as it spat out the words—*unite the self with emptiness; rejoice in eternal purity*. My body twitched spasmodically as I released a hot jet of sperm, but Aya-chan didn't give up her relentless ministrations. She rubbed her finger up and down the seminal duct on the underside of my member, seeking to suck out the last drop. I had come to a place outside the real world: a cold place.

Aya-chan had opened the refrigerator and was drinking a beer. I lay there like a rotten log, sucked dry. Why would she do so much for somebody like me? I looked up and saw her sitting in a chair, wearing only a white shirt. Her legs were drawn up, both feet on the seat; she was balancing the beer glass on her knee, with her genitals exposed. I sat down in the chair across from her. She reached behind her and poured me a glass of beer. As I watched the foam rising, I told myself that I was sitting in a place from which there was no return. Having discharged its load of sperm, the orifice in my member was gaping; the little opening in the glans was breathing in the cold air flowing out of the air-conditioner. I took the postal-savings passbook out of my travel bag and handed it to her. She looked first at the figures written in it, then at me, and laughed.

"You're pretty sorry, you know—coming up with something like this."

"Oh, no, don't get me wrong, please."

"You giving this to me?"

"I guess so—"

"You're pitiful, you know it? It's just empty pride, offering me something like this. Don't make me laugh."

"It's all I've got."

"Yeah, well . . . at least you have this much. Ever since I was a kid, life's been a whole lot tougher for me."

"I see—But this is all I have." I pulled my trousers over, took out the brown paper envelope Seiko Nēsan had given me, and poured out its contents on the table. It was twenty-odd thousand yen and a little more, including a few ten-yen and one-yen coins. "Now, this really is everything."

"I want you to know my brother's sold me for ten million yen."

I was speechless.

"He's already picked up half of that. If I don't show up in Hakata on the twentieth, he's dead. Do you think this pocket change's going to do any good?"

I clasped my hands in front of my face and looked down. I felt like praying.

"I don't want to go to Hakata. If I go, my brother will get the other five million and won't have to die, but I'll be trapped because of the money. Every day I'll have to do what I just did for you, shot up full of speed, and keep it up till I'm an old rag."

I kept my face down. My fists were clenched. I couldn't look at her face. I had the feeling I should be atoning for some transgression of my own.

"What do you expect me to do with this little bit of money? You know it's not going to do any good, don't you?"

"I'm sorry. I came to Ama and—"

"Oh, Seiko Nēsan already told me what to expect. She said I could come back to Ama when I pay off the debt with my body. She was a hooker around here when she was young, you know. But if I go to Hakata, I know I'm going to wind up in the gutter.

I'll end up just like that old whore who does the weird chanting at night in the apartment next to yours—clinging to some man and babbling in tongues."

I looked at Aya-chan's face. She turned away. She seemed to be trying to hold back tears. Her vulva was still facing me. The cold current from the air conditioner was swirling around my shoulders and raising goose bumps on my skin.

"I bet they're going crazy looking for me about now, but I'm not going. Hell with 'em."

She wrapped herself in a *yukata*, the unlined cotton kimono that came with the room. I did the same.

"That's all right, isn't it? Don't you think so?"

"Well—"

"You'll run away with me, won't you?" She looked at me.

I swallowed hard.

"You trailed me once, didn't you? I enjoyed that, you know. I thought, 'what a dumb-ass.'" She closed her eyes. That characteristically dark, brooding look came over her face again. It was a distinctly cold expression, not a look of hunger. "But we don't have anywhere left to run."

I supposed if there were, it would have to be somewhere beyond this earthly existence.

"They'll come after us, no matter where we go, to take back that money my brother got from them. They're like chewing gum sticking to the sole of your shoe."

I clasped my hands in front of my face again and gritted my back teeth. Sanada's voice from this morning echoed in my head. His shouts had come from the depths of his living soul. The summer light glittered on the waves in Osaka Bay. But I couldn't bring myself to accept the reality of the two of us being about to die. Why had she asked me to put on the condom? I took a beer out of the refrigerator and poured some into her glass, then into mine. The rising white foam terrified me no end.

23

Aya-chan was already about to leave when I woke up. She was standing there holding her big cloth handbag. Hurriedly I started to pull myself together.

"I was going to leave by myself," she said.

"Why?"

"You were so sound asleep."

The passbook and cash were still where I'd put them on the table last night. It looked like a pitiful little pile of trash. As Aya-chan left the room, I hastily gathered it up and followed.

There was a diner on the way to the train station. We ordered breakfast, which came with a raw egg. The woman running the shop watched us with a knowing smile; no doubt quite a few couples stopped in here on their way out of the lovers' hotels around this neighborhood. Aya-chan stirred up the raw egg, poured it on top of her rice with some dried seaweed, and started eating. I couldn't eat my raw egg. When I finished eating, the egg was still there.

"Don't you want it?" she asked.

"No. I can't."

She took my egg, cracked it into the bowl, and swallowed it

all at once. It was the same thing the woman at the sundries shop next to the alley in Deyashiki had done in front of my eyes. The same mouth had drained me of semen last night. There was lipstick on the rim of the bowl. Where had she planned to go after leaving me asleep in the hotel room? She had paid the hotel bill, too. The broken halves of the eggshell gaped in the bottom of the bowl. Maybe she didn't want to take me along because she felt sorry for me.

I paid the tab at the diner, the Tarafuku—the "Good and Plenty." After we left, we walked on without any particular destination. The buzzing of the cicadas in the plane trees along the street was earsplitting. Some of the shops had evidently chosen to take their O-Bon holiday late and were still closed. Aya-chan's deadline was August 20; I wondered if she planned to stay hidden in this area until that date passed. If she did, Sanada would be a dead man.

She couldn't go back to Ama if that happened, of course. I wondered who would do the job on Sanada—would it be his own gang or the ones who had advanced him the five million? Either way, Aya-chan would still be a target: the gang whose ten million yen Sanada had squandered would want her to come up with the remaining five million, and those he got the first five from would search for her all the more relentlessly, knowing they'd been taken. We came to Shitennōji Temple. It was a grand establishment; its great, red-painted south gate, middle gate, five-storied pagoda, main sanctuary, and lecture hall stood in a single line running from south to north through serene, spacious grounds. The tall edifices reflected the white glare of the summer sun and cast deep shadows on the ground. Worshippers went to and fro in that reflected light; a naked man lay asleep on the bare earth, evidently a homeless drifter. He had a tattoo on his shoulder. From the belfry behind the lecture hall came the sound of the great, deep-voiced bell, ringing for the souls of the dead.

Weeds grew around the edges of the stepping stones in the yard. There was no place for weeds to grow here except right next to where people trod. When I showed Aya-chan my pass-book last night, she couldn't help laughing out loud at the paltry sum it represented. It had given me some release for a moment, but later I once again felt a kind of guilt. I joined Aya-chan, who had squatted down under the broad eaves of a temple building to get out of the sun.

"It's quiet," she said. "It's nice." A woman carrying a parasol walked by in front of us. "When we were little, my brother and I used to play in a temple yard in Ama, catching earth spiders."

"You mean the kind that lives in these narrow tunnels?"

"Yeah. They dig burrows under the foundation stones, places like that, with a little hole on top of the ground. They spin a white web. We'd roll them up with a thin slip of bamboo or something and catch the spiders that way."

"I've done that, too. The spider holes I was digging around in were by the wall of a house, though, not at a temple. The old lady who lived there would yell at me that I was undermining the house."

"The priest chewed out my brother, too."

"Yeah?"

"I was fast on the getaway, but he was always a screwup."

An ant crawled up on the tip of my wooden clog. We moved over to the stairs in front of the temple and sat down on the lowest step. A breeze was blowing, but it was hot summer air.

"Show me your passbook again, would you?"

I started to pull it out of my bag. Aya-chan's panties, wrapped in newspaper, were in there. The newspaper smelled of raw meat. She glanced at the numbers in the passbook and looked back at me.

"So you want to give me this?"

"I guess so—"

"You sure?"

I took my cheap seal out of the bag and held it out in front of her. "I'm a loser."

"That's all right. Actually, I like losers."

She laughed. I still couldn't bring myself to want to go somewhere with her to die, though. She looked at me for a while with her mouth pursed, as if sucking on a plum pit, then put the passbook and seal away in her handbag. That left me pretty much cleaned out; all I had left was the little bit of cash in my pocket that Seiko Nēsan had given me. I suddenly remembered the dead zelkova bonsai in the window back at the apartment.

"Did you like me doing things like that for you?"

"What?"

She was talking about our lovemaking last night, of course. I had a thirsty feeling.

"If you like it, I'll do it for you all you want. I'm the *kalavinka*, the paradise bird. Besides, I'm the kind of woman who'd take you for all the money in your passbook."

"That's all right. The money's no use to me anyway."

"But what are you going to do starting tomorrow if you don't have it?"

I looked at her face. Her eyes were closed. I closed mine, too. Was she saying this because she thought there would still be a tomorrow if we escaped from this world? Or was she planning to go on and leave me behind? Was it just a word game?

"Uh—"

"What?"

"No—never mind." I was afraid to put it into words and question her outright.

"When I came upstairs that night . . . you were shaking, weren't you?"

"Well, I was surprised."

"I wonder if I really did the right thing, coming upstairs like that."

"Oh, no. I was glad you did."

"Seiko Nēsan used to say you were so square you could make pickles spoil. I found out she was right, you know. When I told you to stand up and did a job on you, your knees were knocking." She giggled.

I had nothing to say.

"Mayu was starting to suspect how I felt. That's why I came up to see you. He's dangerous."

"I suppose so."

"Yeah. The way he throws those razor blades is really scary. He puts them between his fingers, like this, and flips them sideways. He never misses. He can hit a chicken in the eye—a live, moving chicken."

"Yes, I saw that, just once, in the temple yard back in Ama."

"If he finds out I came upstairs, there's no telling what he'll do; he's jealous as hell. It'll be bad news for you and me both. I was terrified after that, wondering how you'd act. I tried as hard as I could to pretend nothing happened."

"I was on pins and needles every day, too, of course."

"I think he suspected something about me going upstairs. I got chills up and down my back every now and then when I thought about him catching on . . . did he say anything to you, try to get something out of you?"

"No. Nothing." I lied, if unintentionally, on the spur of the moment.

"Good, then. If he knew I was here now, he'd come after me no matter what. He's mean and persistent—like a snake."

"I see . . . "

"That's how I wound up wearing something like this on my back, you know."

"Wasn't it something you wanted?"

"Hell, no. Who would? He drove me crazy, pestered me, begged me, ambushed me, got me in a corner where I couldn't get away, then . . . "

"Ah—"

"The night I went up to see you, I was feeling like I really didn't give a damn if he found out. I just wanted to show him up—throw it in his face, just to see how he looked."

If this was so, I wondered what hidden agenda was behind his sending me to Daimotsu to deliver that gun the day before yesterday.

"But you know, when I thought about what kind of trouble I might get you in if I went upstairs . . . "

I said nothing.

"I was lonesome. Mayu told me he decided to send Shimpei to stay with somebody he knew in Gojō. He was even starting to sound like he was tired of me—saying he was thinking about going off again by himself on a trip to work on his skills. I found out later that he already knew about my brother stepping in shit. He was starting to talk like that because he didn't want any of it coming back on him, but I was still clueless. He doesn't need me anymore since he's finished jabbing me with his needles. I'm like an old, used-up toothbrush to him. But if he knew about you and me—that's a different story. He'd follow us all the way to hell to get back at us. Sticking in that needle's all that matters to him. Once he's through with the needle, it's like drinking stale tea to him. Of course, before he started he was saying stuff like 'let me carve my soul into you,' with a face like this." She made a fierce, demonic grimace. "His soul's a hundred-yen stamp. He said there's a temple up north in a place called Hiraizumi, and there's some kind of hanging metal ornament in it with this design, and they put it on the stamp. It didn't make any sense to me."

"So, has Mayu-san been to Hiraizumi?"

"I wanted you to suck my nipples, sweetheart. I wanted you to lick my hairy slit."

The sunlight reflecting off the ground beyond the deep eaves was intensely bright. The five-storied pagoda was casting a dark shadow.

"We say we're human beings, but we're just animals in a human skin. You were shaking that night. Am I that scary a woman?"

"As I said before—"

"All right. That's enough."

A stray dog was wandering around with its red tongue hanging out.

"I'm the kind of woman that would take you for all you got. I just like your little prick, that's all. That's all there is, and that's all I am."

"No. That's not right."

"What? How so?"

"Well, what I mean is . . . "

Our lovemaking that night had unmistakably been a loathsome act, the copulation of beasts. But both Aya-chan and I had been desperate for the chance. We had thirsted for it, and we couldn't resist it. Aya-chan clung to me, and I to her, even as I struggled to shake off my trembling. Neither of us could have stopped it.

"I'm a bought woman, and that means I'm not myself anymore. I'm a dead person, a piece of goods that's bought and sold for money. Kill me or let me live, cook me and eat me like the pork and beef you used to skewer, it's all the same to me. I'm a dead person; it's my ghost talking to you like this now. What am I talking about? Talking about liking your little prick. What a dumb bitch."

"No, you're a lotus blossom—a good woman." I had addressed her just now, for the first time, as *anata*—the polite second-person pronoun. I did it unthinkingly, but somehow it had become inevitable. The words she was speaking were the words of someone who'd become submerged in the darkest depths of this world. There was a sad, angry frigidity in her words that could only emanate from someone who despaired of being human. Inadvertently I had referred to that frigidity as a lotus blossom, but I could just as well have said it was the tattooed *kalavinka* dancing above that flower. I supposed that Horimayu-san's frigidity was so deeply soaked into his own body and soul that in his own way he'd carved it into her flesh, and she was suffering the curse of his frozen spirit. When he'd finished tattooing, however—

Tears were welling up in Aya-chan's eyes. "Men all tell you the same thing. I guess I'm the lotus flower from the village with the muddy ditch. As soon as I got old enough, my brother's friends and a lot of other guys started hitting on me, hanging around like flies. Your prick wasn't behaving either, was it? It said it wanted a piece of me, too, and came chasing after me."

A procession of monks dressed in elaborate vestments came

marching across the temple yard. More than half of them were wearing glasses.

"I've had enough. I've eaten all the muddy soup I could ever stand. Flowers shrivel up sooner or later, you know. Trees keep on getting bigger, of course. My brother wanted to get big, too, when he took the gang's money."

Another column of monks came up. They seemed to be involved in some sort of ceremony following O-Bon. The wail of a siren traversed the midday sky, probably signaling noon.

We left the temple compound and walked on. There were a lot of temples in this neighborhood. The dense stands of trees around them were full of the buzz of cicadas. Then there was a whole row of motorcycle shops. Coming to Matchamachi Street, we grabbed some steamed meat dumplings and beer at a cheap Chinese restaurant at the bottom of the hill and then ate some fried rice. For Aya-chan, the beer, dumplings, and rice were no doubt just more mud-flavored stew. The name of the little eatery was the Shanghai. After I finished eating, I went to the toilet to defecate. When I came back, I saw no sign of her. A chill shot through me. When I grabbed some money out of my pocket, the waiter said, "It's been paid for, sir." I ran outside, and the brilliant sun dazzled my eyes. Aya-chan was standing at the bottom of the hill, looking up at some oleander flowers. The beer I had just drunk was bursting out from every pore of my body. Suddenly I was seized by a violent lust. I wanted to attach myself to Aya-chan's breast. Now I was definitely even more infatuated with her than when I got off at Tennōji Station the night before. Or maybe she was beginning to take on a life of her own inside me, and that's what the last chill was about.

We started walking uphill, along the street. The midsummer sun was fierce. There was a darkness in the depths of my eyes.

We had no idea where we were going. The cicadas were making a racket. Nothing was moving, though, and our surroundings were still; our shadows were the only things in motion. As I walked along staring at those shadows, it seemed to me as though the two of us were drifting in a void.

We came to the grounds of a temple dedicated to Rāgarāja— the patron god of lovers and prostitutes. There was nobody around. Like the other temples, the woodwork on this building was painted vermilion. There were a lot of oleanders here, too; pink and white flowers seemed to spill over in their clusters. I walked into the shadow of the temple. Aya-chan stayed standing on the paving stones in the middle of the courtyard, staring at the front of the building. Her hands were limp by her sides. The intense sunshine put a glow in her hair. She kept staring at the latticework shutters on the temple façade. She wasn't praying. She was burning herself up as she stood in the midst of the light. I approached her through the light.

"You know, I saw a guy getting packed in concrete in a barrel once."

"What?"

"He was crying, hollering for help. He used to think he was some kind of big shot, too."

I swallowed hard.

"They're going to do my brother that way, too. He sold me off, but he only has half the money. Of course he already gave that to the gang, so he can't return it either. Both sides are going to be after him. It's all over."

The white light was stinging.

"I guess that barrel's still at the bottom of Akashi Strait."

"Was it somebody you knew?"

"Yeah. He used to follow me around."

I was speechless.

"I didn't pay him any attention, but he threw himself around and showed off. Driving a foreign car and stuff. Even drove it down the street just to buy a pack of cigarettes. Asking me if I wanted to go for a ride . . . hell, I'd just as soon have a guy that's broke."

No wonder Horimayu-san got the urge to carve a lotus flower tattoo into her back. It must have seemed to him as if the paradise bird were flying over Ama, the city with no human vitality.

Leaving the temple, we went down the hill along the stone fence of a Shinto shrine and wound up at Tennōji Park. On the high ground to the left was the grand edifice of the Osaka City Museum of Art. To the right was the zoo; beyond the zoo we could see Tsūtenkaku, a steel observation structure that mimicked the Eiffel Tower. Drifters were sleeping naked in the shade of the trees in the park landscape or sitting motionless as they watched the men and women wandering beneath the summer sun. I would be like that in a few days. But would I really be wandering in this world those few days? I already felt dead as I wandered through this world in the light.

"Those people are sleeping on flattened cardboard boxes, aren't they?" she said.

"Yes, they are. In winter they make shelters out of them to sleep in."

"The trash business has a word for those boxes. They're called *gotashin*. I know, because I grew up in a ragpickers' slum, with trash all around. You could get top prices for that stuff back then, but it's no good these days. There's so much paper everywhere, most recycling people don't want it any more. I used to play every day in the boxes my mom brought home. Kids like to get inside boxes, don't they?"

"I guess so."

"I used to like to get into a box and then have my mom or my brother close it up so I couldn't get out. I was a funny little girl, wasn't I?"

I gave a silent laugh.

"At first my brother would just mess around, get up on the box and stuff, but after I stayed quiet inside for so long he'd start worrying about me little by little, and then he'd call through a crack in the box: "Ayako! Ayako!""

"I see."

"But I wouldn't answer, so he'd go away for a while, but then he'd come right back. I had him pegged, you know; I knew he was the kind of guy who wouldn't give up on me. He'd always come right back. He'd go away, but he'd worry and worry and couldn't get the box out of his mind. He can't even pretend he doesn't care."

"So he never just left you alone?"

"Never. My brother's not that kind of guy. He looks tough, but he doesn't have the guts. He'd call my name—"Ayako!"— and open the box for me every time."

There was no father in her family, I was sure.

We went into the zoo. It was the first time I had gone into one since reaching adulthood; Aya-chan said it was the same with her. I thought there might be a lot of families there with children since it was summer vacation, but there were only a few visitors. I supposed not many people wanted to walk around in a place like this in the hot sun. I probably wouldn't have gone in either if I hadn't been drifting in the void like that. More than half the other visitors were either couples past the age of reproduction, accompanied by the fruits of their reproductive activity, or young couples in heat who'd come to breathe the rank odors of gluttony and lust given off by these beasts, birds, and reptiles as they prepared to go forth and multiply.

The penguins were getting a shower with water from a hose held by a zookeeper. The ostriches were holding their long necks still. The hippo was submerged in the water with only its eyes showing. A gorilla sat motionless in his cage, with folded arms. The tiger lay flat on its belly, overcome by the heat. The giraffe stood stock-still in the hot sun with its tongue sticking out. All these creatures were "merchandise," bought with money, condemned to live until they die.

The scene was no different from the one I saw when I was first taken to the zoo at Himeji Castle Park, but there was one difference: my way of seeing these living things had changed. I could no longer enjoy looking at them. The *kalavinka* walking along beside me was another creature bought and sold with money. I felt a pain inside me.

We went into a rest house and got a cold drink. Aya-chan went to the toilet. When she came back, she asked me, "Why'd you come to Ama?"

"I quit my job without any idea of what I was going to do from then on. When winter came two years later, I didn't even have a sweater."

"But if you were in that kind of shape, why couldn't you just get a job with another company?"

"Well, there was that, but . . . the oil crisis came along, the world was all topsy-turvy . . . when you play *hanafuda*, don't you sometimes suddenly go bust when you think you're about to win because you've got zero, the lowest hand possible and you haven't pulled the last card? There's a trick like that in two-ten-jack, too."

"That's a tough hand. Wow—do you play *hanafuda*?"

"Oh, I've played two or three times."

"That hand's only got a ten-thousand-to-one chance of winning, you know. You always end up pulling a card at the end that makes you go bust. You don't want it, but it's fixed so you have to draw a card, and that last card's waiting to wipe you out. There's a word for going out with the lowest hand, isn't there? You wanted to do that, didn't you?"

"Yes, I did—but I pulled that card and went bust in the end."

"Now I understand. You . . . "

"Well no, I just pulled a card I didn't need."

I felt as though I had let something slip out. Nevertheless, it was true: I had once wished for the winning hand in life.

We left the zoo. It was already past four thirty. Time seemed to have started to go by at an accelerating pace. I wondered where we were to go. Right in front of us, grimy Tsūtenkaku tower reared up toward the sky. The district was teeming with businesses: clothing shops with outmoded readymade outfits on the racks, cheap bars reeking of grilled organ meat. I had heard rumors that dog meat could be found in the stews served around here; it would have been no surprise, considering the diseased beef and pork I'd been handling back in Deyashiki. Huge paper lanterns shaped like fugu hung in front of a restaurant serving dishes that featured the puffer fish. In front of a cheap theater stood gaudy banners advertising a second-rate traveling kabuki company. Along the street, people clustered around benches where *shōgi* players sat hunched over their games of chess; a kibitzer, gnawing a fried pork cutlet on a stick, peered over the shoulders of the crowd. The whole street scene was dingy, its dinginess mercilessly exposed in the intense summer afternoon sun.

"Hey, Aya-chan! Is that you?" The man who called out wore a mesh shirt and sported a head of short, kinky, permanent-waved hair. I could sense Aya-chan drawing a startled breath.

"What the hell are you doing here?" she asked him.

He looked at me and leered knowingly. I could tell at a glance that he was a *kusubori*.

"Your brother showed up at the office today—a little after lunchtime, actually. He looked kind of gray in the face."

"Really? Is he still there?"

"No, he's gone now. I don't know what it was about, but he was in back talking to the boss until just a little while ago. Right after that, seems like, Horimayu-san came in. So you weren't with him?"

He rubbed his nose with his finger and shot me a sharp glance. I felt Aya-chan sucking in her breath again.

"Coming all the way down here in this miserable heat—you enjoying yourselves?"

"Sure. I wanted to see the zoo one time," she said.

"The zoo? Well, that's . . . "

"Yeah. I like ostriches. You know, they lay eggs this big."

"Oh . . . "

"Well, see you around."

Aya-chan turned on her heel and walked off. The man looked at me. All the hair on my body seemed to be standing on end. I quickly followed after Aya-chan. Fear struck me: not only Sanada, but Horimayu-san too had turned up so close. In my mind I saw the gleam of the pistol I delivered in Daimotsu, two days before, to the man named Saitō. We walked on toward ever-livelier stretches of street. Aya-chan said nothing, and neither did I. We were walking fast; the blood was coursing fiercely through my body, as if about to boil.

My time alone with Aya-chan had been shattered. I had no idea where we were or where we were going. Certainly we were no longer just drifting in a void, but nothing we passed caught my attention—not the street scenery, not the faces of people we passed. It felt as though the whole street were gyrating wildly; at the same time I was seized with a raw feeling of actuality, as though the void had suddenly turned real. The raw memory of that man's little finger and its missing end joint, rubbing his nose, kept coming back to me.

All of a sudden we arrived at a spot where we could see Tennōji Station. Aya-chan stopped for a moment, then walked on toward the station. The evening shadows were already closing in. Once inside the station, she went straight over to the temporary storage lockers. These lockers were in the Kintetsu Railway part of the station, not the loop line part where I had stowed my things. Aya-chan pulled a large suitcase out of one of the lockers.

"What are you going to do?" she asked.

"Well . . . "

She fixed her eyes on me. They didn't move. They had a fearsome sense of presence.

"I don't have anywhere to go," I said.

"Then you'll come along with me?"

"Sure. Take me with you."

"Where are we going?"

I was silent. I bit my lip. She was still looking at me. I had the panicky feeling that I needed to say something.

"Why don't we go to that place there for our final stop tomorrow?" she said.

I turned around and saw on the wall behind me a tourist poster for the Forty-Eight Waterfalls of Akamé. Water was rushing over rapids in a forest. A small boy in a white summer hat was standing in front of them, with his back to us, holding a white insect net. As a boy I, too, had run across hills and fields with an insect net.

My voice shook as I answered. "Yes. That looks like a nice place."

Aya-chan's words "for our final stop" dwelled on the tip of my tongue. So we were going to cross over, from one world to the next.

We started walking along the street again. I was carrying my things, too, wrapped up in a cloth. We went along the darkest streets we could find. We went into a bar called Takoya. It seemed like a mom-and-pop place, a little rundown. The only other customers were three men who looked like low-ranking civil servants. Finding seats in the back hidden behind a column, we ordered some chopped octopus and raw fish. As we each downed an icy beer, the fatigue of a whole day's walk in the hot sun seemed to fall away.

When the guy back at the zoo mentioned Sanada's "gray" face, it reminded me of the voice I'd heard the morning before, back in Deyashiki. I hadn't told Aya-chan yet about Sanada coming to look for her that morning. I also hadn't told her about Seiko Nēsan coming by, two days before that. If I did, the message I'd be delivering would be "go to Hakata." Just the mention of that "gray face," I'm sure, gave Aya-chan a clear sense of Sanada's desperation. On top of that, Horimayu-san was wandering around looking for us. The intensity of the shock was clear in Aya-chan's subsequent words and behavior—like an ostrich running. Still, the idea that this was our last night had not yet become real in my mind, even if Sanada's "gray face" and Horimayu-san's icy glare were making their mark with every step we took. The deadline was tomorrow: August 20.

"His name's Teramori. I'll bet he'll tell Mayu he saw us coming out of the zoo together," she said.

"Most likely he will."

"That's all right. It doesn't matter."

I didn't reply.

"My poor brother. He's desperate to find me, but damned if I'm going to Hakata."

We both fell silent. It felt like I was going deaf. I began to feel again as though I should say something. "Let's do go to Akamé tomorrow," I said.

Aya-chan looked me in the eyes. Silence fell again. I breathed in the quiet atmosphere. We could smell the fish the restaurant woman was grilling. Aya-chan poured herself a beer and then one for me. The foam bubbled. I shut my eyes and downed my beer in one gulp. It seemed as though I were swallowing my own fate.

I told Aya-chan about the episode when Shimpei threw the rock at me.

"Oh, so that's what it was." She laughed. "He's sort of like Mayu in some funny ways."

Shimpei's ruined origami pieces came to mind. "What happened to his mother?" I asked.

"I don't know either. That's one thing Mayu never told me."

"I see."

"I did hear some rumors."

"For instance?"

"Like she ran off with his best friend. The kind of thing you hear all the time. Actually, what I heard was she and this guy were an item to begin with, but she had Shimpei with Mayu while the other guy was on the inside. That's what Seiko Nēsan told me, anyway."

"Inside where?"

"Oh, come on. You know what I mean." Aya-chan smiled a faint, meaningful smile.

I figured it meant behind bars. She was knocking back the cold saké she'd ordered. She poured me one after another, too; the time passed quickly like that.

We walked along dark streets until we came to the grounds of Ikutama Shrine, where I relieved myself. The arc of urine took on the color of the garish neon lights nearby. There were lovers' hotels all around the shrine; we checked into a place called Napoli. We were drunker than we'd been the night before. We tumbled onto the bed in each other's arms, but we reeked of sweat; right away we went and showered together. I lathered up Aya-chan's body and scrubbed, determined to uncover her very soul. The colors of the tattoo on her back seemed to grow more vibrant; it moved like some animal with an existence of its own. After we finished showering, we cooled off in front of the air-conditioner and each drank another mouthful of beer.

Then she came straight out with it: "Well, it's nothing but memories now, right?"

"What?"

"What I said was, you and I are sitting here like this, but it's all over now—nothing left but memories. Isn't that right?"

I said nothing.

Aya-chan put down her glass and pulled the telephone over.

"Ah, Seiko Nēsan? It's me, Ayako . . . No, I can't tell you that . . . Oh, I see. My brother's gone? . . . Why do I have to go to Hakata? Why don't you go? . . . What about tomorrow? Don't give me that crap. Why don't you just go tomorrow? . . . You can turn the tricks and give 'em back their money . . . What? No, I can't tell you. Oh, by the way, I saw Teramori-san today . . . Where am I? Damn if I'm telling you . . . Su-yeong? Sure, she's just a baby, and it's tough on you, but why should I go? Don't be silly! . . . All right. Bye."

Aya-chan hung up. The deadline was tomorrow, August 20. I could feel the stress. She took off her bathrobe and got on the bed, her naked body sprawling across the sheets. She reached out a hand and dimmed the light. The tattoo looked like a huge, ugly bruise. Her breasts shook as she rolled over.

24

It was after eight the next morning when we left the hotel. Uehonmachi Station on the Kintetsu line was nearby, but Aya-chan wanted to go farther, to Tsuruhashi Station on the National Railways loop line. We walked down the gently sloping street. There was a hamburger place next to the station, where we ate without sitting down.

After we finished, she said to me, "I have to do just one more thing before we go on to Akamé."

"Which is . . . ?"

"You know where I got this bag out last night? At Tennōji Station? I want you to go there and wait for me. It's before nine now. I promise I'll be there by eleven thirty."

"Well—"

I was puzzled. I wondered if she was planning to stand me up and leave me in the lurch, and it showed on my face.

"What's worrying you? Just trust me and wait. All right?"

She turned her back on me and left the shop. I followed, but she immediately grabbed a waiting taxi, shooting a glance toward me as she got in. I could see her head over the backseat as the cab drove off.

It had been barely a minute since we were wolfing down our hamburgers. The cold look in her eyes as she glanced back stung me. The August sky overhead was a deep blue. I felt as if I'd been thrown into an utterly alien pocket of time.

Abruptly I recalled the scene at Yotsuya Station when Masako turned her back on me and left, saying, "Well, that's it." I told myself at the time she was running away from me; it might also have been the moment when something disappeared from within me.

Aya-chan was a stranger, too. I was sure that stresses totally incomprehensible to me were constantly working in her mind. The words she'd spoken to me two nights before breathed on their own, tangling in my mind: the cries of the man dumped into Akashi Strait in a barrel of concrete, Aya-chan's hushed breathing inside the discarded cardboard box—

I started walking along the street beside the elevated railroad tracks. Tennōji Station was the third one down. Aya-chan had tried to leave without me yesterday morning, probably because she didn't want to get me involved; her state of mind after running into that Teramori character was definitely not normal. I, too, felt threatened. When she mentioned wanting to go to the Akamé Falls "for our final stop," the look in her eyes penetrated my heart. But where had she gone all of a sudden? To Hakata? If so, it was all over. Surely not.

Or maybe she'd gone to "the office" where Teramori's gang hung out. If so, she'd probably never be able to come back. It didn't matter: I'd have to keep waiting no matter what. Hadn't I seen the lotus blossom that looked like an ugly burn scar? Hadn't I caressed it? Maybe she was telling me, "run while you've got the chance." But the *kalavinka*'s eyes were terrible:

the paradise bird's eyes had been fixed on me. I had nowhere left to go.

As the station clock's hands approached 11:40, I began to think I didn't care whether she came or not. I was losing my patience. If she wasn't coming, there must be some reason for it. The longer I waited, the more tired and impatient I got, and I became obsessed with the thought of taking her life; I was consumed with the desire to throw myself, with her, into a deep pool at the bottom of the Forty-Eight Falls of Akamé. If she did show up, I was certain we'd wind up wandering on to "the end." It was frightening.

> But please don't be afraid
> And get that hat for me.

It felt as if I were going deaf again. I wanted to run.

Aya-chan came running up in little steps. "Sorry you had to wait."

"No problem—"

Her nose was sweaty, and she was panting. She was carrying a large suitcase. "I was so glad when I saw you from back there."

I said nothing.

"When I got into the cab, I felt like I couldn't blame you if you decided not to wait for me here. But I had to go, no matter what."

"Oh, no, I—"

"I'm sorry. You did wait for me after all, didn't you? Thanks. I'll never forget it." She was talking breathlessly in a way that was unusual for her. She was totally wrapped up in herself, not concerned about what I might have been thinking while standing around waiting for her. Until just moments before, the more I thought about killing this woman, the more I'd also wanted to cut and run. I felt a sudden urge to scream.

"Let's put the baggage in here." She put a coin in the locker slot. "You put your stuff in there, too. You're not going to need that any more, are you?"

I had no idea what she had in that suitcase, but all I had in my bundle was some underwear and things like that. We had both changed into fresh underwear last night; we didn't need to worry about any more changes. Aya-chan pulled out the key.

We took the loop line to Tsuruhashi Station. The Kintetsu train to Akamé would leave from there. We jumped on the express from Tsuruhashi to Nabari at 12:40 p.m. on August 20. As the train left the station, the cluttered townscape of Osaka came into view. I supposed this would be our last sight of such scenery in this life. Everything was clear and sharp: the roofs, walls, billboards, the glitter of leaves on the trees, the streets white in the hot sun, the cars, people, elementary school kids, oleander flowers, the summer weeds growing in vacant lots.

And yet I felt no particular emotion. My mind was like a dull lump. A young woman, twenty-five or -six, and a thirty-four-year-old man in wooden geta clogs, sitting silently on the long bench seat: that was all. At least that was all as it must have looked to the other people on the train.

We're on our way to die. We're going to commit double sui-cide. We're going to the Forty-Eight Falls of Akamé. We're running away to the other world. Anybody who wants to can sit in the seats on this train. We bought tickets so we

*could sit in these seats. You bought tickets so you could, too.
But our seats are ours alone. Where are all of you going?
To your poor old aunt's? On company business to pull the
wool over someone's eyes? To go lose a soccer match? To
a friend's house to apologize? Soon you'll be leaving those
seats, won't you? But we've taken our seats. We can't leave
them. We can't give them up to anybody. Our seats go to the
Forty-Eight Falls of Akamé. There are no seats for a return
trip. Anybody can sit in these seats, but they're the ones we
alone sat in. They're golden seats. See? Aren't they glowing
right here? These are the seats of death.*

I was saying these things to myself. The more I said, however, the more the words rang hollow. There wasn't any golden
glow. Aya-chan was holding my hand, caressing my fingertips.
It was the first time anybody had ever done something like that
to me in public. My mind was occupied by the somehow flus-
tered happiness she had shown when she arrived to meet me
at Tennōji Station. She hadn't expected me to wait for her. I
wondered where she had been. Within her was a whole world
unknown to me, but she must have been honestly happy I had
waited for her.

"Seiko Nēsan—did you know she was from Nabari?" Nabari
was in a district once known as Iga Province—hence the Igaya,
the name of her shop.

"Oh, of course."

"She loves a flower that grows in the Iga mountains—they
call it *mushikari*. She decorated her shop with some of them
again this year. It's a white flower that grows on a shrub. And
she gave me some fringed dianthus once. She said she'd picked

them in the mountains around Nabari. They were white, too. She comes across like a sour old bitch, but she can be different like that."

"That's right. I—" I was going to tell her about getting the bonsai from Seiko Nēsan, but somehow the words wouldn't come. Seiko Nēsan's life must have been like a trampled white flower that gradually turned to straw.

"She thought of you like her own kid, you know," she said.

"Really?—"

"Didn't a friend of yours come from Tokyo to find you? She was talking about that, too."

"He just wanted to come see what kind of fix I was in, that's all."

"But didn't he come because he was worried about you? He took all that trouble. When a little girl jumps rope with a long rubber band, she hollers, 'Look! Look!' People want other people to see."

I said nothing.

"But when you've got real problems, you can't open up to anybody else. As long as you can talk to people about it, you're not really in trouble, are you? Of course I came running to you, didn't I? I felt like you made me alive again."

She laughed. The green of the woods and fields outside the train windows glowed in the blazing summer sun. A woman who looked like a farm wife sat right in front of us; she'd taken a thermos of water and some bread out of her backpack and was eating.

It was an ordinary, everyday scene inside a suburban train. Aya-chan and I were just sitting there side by side. Yet sitting there side by side felt like a different kind of reality, just out of reach. I, at least, hadn't forgotten my urge to run away while waiting there back at the station. My heart had jumped when Aya-chan appeared. Something dreadful was coming toward me. And we were on this train.

Still, being on the train seemed no more than an unreal version of reality. Outside the windows the Yamato region passed by, one summer scene of mountains and valleys after another. Aya-chan's eyes were glowing in that summer light. Every cell of her body gave off an air of joy about "going to die with Ikushima-san." No, it may have been an air of sorrow at having her back covered in ink. In my head, I reenacted our lovemaking over and over. Above the lotus blossom, the *kalavinka* writhed with its wings outspread.

The train arrived at Akamé Station. The station plaza was full of midday light and shade. We were hungry, but the local transit bus was already waiting. There were only a few passengers, including us. A woman with a parasol stood at the edge of the station plaza, unmoving. I looked back at Aya-chan; she was staring straight ahead. I was startled by the look in her eyes, sensing something abnormal in it. The cheerful mood I'd noticed a while ago in the train was now totally gone. There was nobody in the street in front of us. The summer light fell on a serene stretch of ground. The look in Aya-chan's eyes told me she was probably staring death directly in the face. The woman with the parasol came into view again; at the same instant, the bus started off.

In about twenty minutes, we arrived at a facility called the Akamé Tourist House. It was a cluttered-looking place in the midst of some nondescript woods. We finished a bottle of beer as we waited for our bowls of fried pork and rice. Aya-chan had practically quit taking notice of anything since we got on the bus. She was paying no attention to me, either, just staring straight ahead as if at something somewhere beyond. The beer seemed to have lost its flavor. I had the feeling this would be our last taste of food and drink, but had no strong desire to eat.

According to my watch, it was a little before three in the afternoon. It seemed to me the watch's hands had slowed down considerably. I kept having the urge to say something, but couldn't find the words.

Finishing the last of the beer, Aya-chan spoke to me in a low voice. "I don't think you're up to it."

I looked at her, surprised. She avoided my eyes. Our bowls arrived, but they had no flavor. Somehow we had arrived at Akamé while wandering in the void. Having arrived aroused no sense of awe in me. It had just been a matter of chance—or perhaps some other sort of "matter" had chanced to find its momentum. No doubt I'd come here because that momentum had caught me and hurled me forward.

Aya-chan was silently eating her pork and rice. I wondered why she said, "I don't think you're up to it." Where in her mind had those words come from? I could clearly feel my own mind going cold again. I couldn't eat even half of my meal. Aya-chan reached over with her chopsticks and took some of my leftover pickles. We were going to see the waterfalls next—and then what?

Aya-chan paid the bill at the rest house. Except for breakfast at the diner near Tennōji Station yesterday, she had been paying for everything. The falls seemed to extend quite a distance up the mountain, according to the Forty-Eight Falls tourist map they gave us at the restaurant, although there actually seemed to be only about twenty falls altogether.

We walked up the path along the stream. Perhaps a dozen

people were always in sight, both in front of us and behind. Some had brought children along. The mountains around us were clothed in dense green summer foliage that seemed to swirl in the wind. The path was wet, almost dark in the shade of the trees: cryptomeria, beech, maples, elm, and fir. After the urban heat of Osaka, the air felt refreshing—even a little chilly. Cicadas made a metallic racket.

After we walked a little while, a small waterfall came into view. It was named the Hermit's Fall. Next, the Sacred Serpent's Fall appeared to our left. I surmised from the name that it was connected with some legend, perhaps the one about the White Serpent Princess. As we crossed a bridge, we saw the Fall of Fudō, the blue-faced, fiery Buddhist guardian deity; this was a big one. Behind was a tall cliff, rising straight up like a huge folding screen.

The stream was called the Jōroku-gawa. It was about twelve feet wide. We joined some other people peering into a deep pool and saw a dense school of freshwater bluefish swimming in the clear water. Rapids and curiously-shaped rock formations followed one after another: the Maiden's Waterfall; the Eight-Mat Rock; the Fall of the Thousand-Armed Goddess. The falls went over stepped places in the bedrock following the swiftly flowing stream. The Fall of the Thousand-Armed Goddess was beautiful. A black butterfly flitted across the water. I wanted to hurry on up to where there were no people. Whatever was about to happen, it seemed better for my peace of mind to get somewhere we could be alone as soon as possible. But Aya-chan was the one going ahead at a rapid pace. She walked on and on, without saying a word. She seemed to know exactly where she wanted to go to die.

Aya-chan stopped. She put her hand in the water, picked up

a stone, and threw it back in. I could see the water rippling over the rocks in the streambed; the fish disappeared.

"This is a pretty spot, don't you think?"

"Yes—" The half-heartedness of my reply increased my own irritation.

"My brother was supposed to come here on a school trip when he was in grade school. But we didn't have the money, so Mama pretended to be sick to fool him. She told him to tell the teacher he couldn't come on the trip because he had to look after his sick mama. He was miserable all day. Later on, when she was really sick and about to die, she told me, 'I wasn't fair to Jong-nyeong, and this is my punishment.'"

The sound of the waterfalls seemed to grow louder in my ears.

"But I did get to go on a school trip that day. We went to Mt. Kabuto, near Takarazuka. Now here I am, with you—I thought about my brother's missed trip when we got on the bus a while ago. Memories are hard, aren't they? It's like there's a big hole somewhere."

"Is that the only kind of memories you have?"

"This is a pretty place, but he wouldn't be happy even if he got to come here now. There's no way he'd be happy unless he was back in fifth grade. It's all past and gone now, right? He went for the money because he wanted a better life."

"I suppose so, but—"

"So now I'm here, at a place my brother never made it to. But I wasn't thinking about that when I saw the poster at the station. I'd forgotten all about it. I was in first grade then, after all, you know. But the moment I got on the bus, all of a sudden what Mama said came back to me." "I'm happy I came here with you today," she said.

"Really?—" She seemed to have stopped before saying something she wanted to say.

I wondered if "I don't think you're up to it" meant that I had somehow disappointed her.

A little farther on, we came to a splendid fall called Nunobikidaki. The name meant a long strip of cloth, the image evoked by the tall stream of falling water. It must have been a hundred feet high, and it plunged straight into a dark blue-green pool. It was in a shady fold of the mountain; the river flowed slowly here, swirling deep and dark, the bottom invisible. There were deep stretches like this along the rivers back home. My grandmother had told me there was a cave in the bank below the surface; "a beautiful princess lives there and weaves on her loom," she had said.

Immediately upstream from Nunobikidaki was a deep area called the Dragon's Pool. Water from here cascaded straight down toward Nunobikidaki, directly below. It looked to me like the perfect spot for someone contemplating suicide. The water here ran in a torrent between the rocks. If you slid from here toward the pool at the bottom of the fall, there was no doubt the rocks would crush your skull on the way down.

Maybe Aya-chan was somehow reading my thoughts; she too was staring into the deep water. Of course, now was not the time. People were coming this way from farther upstream. We had been walking for nearly an hour.

I kept on, straight ahead. If she had lost confidence in me, I thought, then I'd be damned if I was going to let her die without me. I felt determined to die. The blood in my veins seemed icy yet ready to boil at any moment.

On the other hand, if she'd given up on me, dying with her now would be meaningless. In fact, no matter how you did it, dying made no more sense than living: after all, life's no more than a blink of light in the darkness. The waterfalls followed one after another, every one of them breathtakingly beautiful, their names colorful, romantic, dramatic. A naked man was bathing in the spray beneath one of them. Late afternoon shadows were already creeping here and there across the mountain.

We arrived at a spot called Hundred-Mat Rock. On top of this huge rock slab was a teahouse. A colorful banner hanging from its eaves advertised flavored ices. Three women customers were in the shop, drinking sodas. The surface of the rock stretched from the front of the teahouse all the way down to the stream. I turned to Aya-chan and was about to ask whether she wanted to rest a minute but immediately held my tongue. She walked on ahead, and I followed without saying a word. Small purple flowers bloomed along the path.

Six more waterfalls, clear and cold, appeared in succession before we reached the one called Ninaidaki. This waterfall was outstandingly handsome; true to its name, which meant "carrying yoke," it was divided left and right by a huge boulder that stood in the middle of the stream. Aya-chan stood silently, gazing at the fall.

A little farther on came a fall stair-stepped like a platform for displaying dolls on Girls' Day. We had nothing left to talk about. As the sun began to sink behind the mountain, the number of people coming back down the path began to dwindle. Time seemed to be pushing us from behind.

It was probably past five o'clock when we came to Biwadaki, the Falls of the Lute. There was no sign of other people. Aya-chan, who had been walking ahead of me, suddenly stopped and turned to look back at me.

"Listen. I've had enough," she said.

"What?" I stared at her. In the cool mountain air of the approaching evening, the whites of her eyes looked almost bluish.

"I can't kill you."

I was speechless.

She bit her lip. "I'd been thinking that I wanted to die with you. I really did. I was so happy when I saw you waiting for me at the station."

The sound of the waterfall was rushing past my ears.

"But now that I've come all the way here with you, I'm satisfied. I can't kill you. I can't take you with me. That's what I thought when I saw you waiting at the station. The whole load fell off my mind right then. I don't want to be the card you draw and go bust. I want you to win. I want you to win with the best hand you've got. Today's August 20. Today's the day. To save my brother, I should be in Hakata right now, but it doesn't matter. They're going to whack him anyway."

I swallowed hard. Aya-chan and I had come here today, and because of that Sanada was going to be killed. No, Aya-chan probably came here only because I'd been waiting at the station in Tennōji. She was telling me she couldn't have come here by herself.

"I need to go back to Osaka now."

My chest was heaving.

"I feel like I treated you wrong. I'm sorry. But I'm really happy, too. I've got to go back to Osaka. You know when I made you wait this morning? I didn't get everything done then that I needed to. I told them you were waiting for me and I'd come back later."

"I see—"

The sound of the waterfall was roaring in my ears. The base

of the fall was like a big rocky outdoor bathing pool, surrounded by sheer cliffs. She must have gone to the office where Teramori and his associates hung out. He'd said yesterday that both San-ada and Horimayu-san had been by there. Horimayu-san must have been looking for her—maybe for both of us. But the fact that Sanada had been there meant something different. It must have been a place Sanada felt he could go for help when there was no other hope. Teramori's attitude toward Aya-chan hadn't been rude. She must have gone there for some kind of help, too.

It was summer, but after all it was the latter part of August. As the sun went down beyond the mountain, the evening shadows began to close in quickly. I moved closer to Aya-chan. I wanted to embrace her, but she gave a little laugh and dodged me, then walked on down the mountain path as I kept my eyes on her back.

The shadows had closed in almost completely by the time we got back to the Dragon's Pool. Aya-chan stopped walking. She stared down into the depths of the stream. The water was dark and slowly swirling. There was no longer another soul around. She looked at me.

"Hold me again," she said.

I could find nothing to say in reply.

As she approached, I was afraid for a moment that she might throw herself into the water with her arms still wrapped around me. She held me in a tight embrace. We stumbled that way, together, onto the mountain path; one of my clogs came off. The waterfall was still roaring in my ears.

By the time we arrived back at the rest house, the sun had set completely. A pole with a light stood amid the stand of trees. The restaurant was already closed. Aya-chan's white dress and my pants were caked with mud and damp leaves from the wet mountain path. Dry leaf fragments were stuck in her hair. We sat on a bench in the woods and waited for the bus. I wondered what would happen if we went back to Osaka. Maybe I might end up living with this woman somewhere out of sight. But wait—what would happen to Sanada? What would Mayu-san do? Things were just going to have to take their course.

"I want you to know something. My name's really Yi Mun-hyong. I'm Korean."

"I know. Seiko Nēsan told me."

"Really? That old lady does like to talk, doesn't she?"

"She's a lonely person."

"Will you go by and see her once in a while for me when you get the chance?"

"Sure. I've got something I need to give her, too."

"What is it?"

"Nothing much."

"Oh, come on. You can tell me, can't you?"

I laughed. The sachet I'd bought in Kyoto was in the inside pocket of my bag. The moon had risen over the valley. When Aya-chan saw it, she said, "I like the moon. I like thunder, too."

Just then, the bus pulled up. Several other people were standing at the bus stop.

It was after 8.00 p.m. when we got on the Kintetsu train at Akamé Station to go back to Osaka. There were only a few passengers. Outside the train window, the lights of the houses went by. Occasionally auto headlights passed in and out of view.

An insect was flying around inside the train car. It collided heavily with a windowpane and fell to the floor. It was a large moth, the pattern on its wings like dry leaves. A well-dressed, fiftyish woman sitting across from us suddenly crushed it beneath her shoe. There was a different feeling about this train trip from when we came out. Of course the fear of trouble when we got back to Osaka, depending on how things went, was still there. But what I'd felt before, the sense of reality being just out of reach, was now gone. Sitting on the train felt like sitting on the train, and that was all. We were no longer wandering lost in the void. We sat surrounded by a sense of relief as fresh as newly split wood.

Aya-chan was leaning against me as if completely exhausted. I was sure she was hungry; I was, and my throat was parched. I began to wonder just what this whole day had meant. The back of my neck ached from fatigue; it felt almost paralyzed. The one thing that had penetrated my mind deeply was the rush of cold water from the waterfalls in the deep woods at Akamé. I stared at the crushed moth. One by one, I counted my breaths as if to make sure I was still alive. The woman in front of us sat there as if nothing had ever happened.

I took the sachet out of my bag. It was wrapped in transparent paper. Aya-chan's eyes were closed; she seemed to have dozed off.

"This is it," I told her. She took it in her hand. "I was planning to give it to Seiko Nēsan."

Aya-chan looked at me.

"It's a sachet," I said.

She gave a sly smile and held the open wrapper up to her nose. "Yeah. Smells nice."

"Does it? Seiko Nēsan did me a lot of favors, after all."

"How about giving it to me?"

"Pardon?"

"You can buy her another one, can't you?" She put the sachet in her own handbag. "I guess I'm just the kind that keeps on taking from you, huh?" she said.

I laughed. The train pulled into Yamato-Yagi Station and stopped. This was the transfer point for the Kashiwara line, which runs north and south. Passengers got on and off. Just then—

"I'm getting off here," Aya-chan announced abruptly, and stood up. "I'm going to Kyoto from here and on to Hakata."

She ran out onto the platform. Immediately I tried to get up and follow, but the toes on one of my feet missed the strap of the wooden clog. Just as I stood up, the train doors closed. My eyes met hers through the window. I swallowed hard. Her eyes were motionless; they seemed to be holding back something terrible. I plastered myself against the door as the train began to move. The palms of my hands were cold. Aya-chan ran five or six steps along the platform toward me, then dropped out of sight.

25

For four years after that, I led a covert existence in the lower-class districts of a succession of cities: Osaka, Sakai, a couple of different neighborhoods in Kobe. The summer I turned thirty-eight, I went back to Tokyo and got another office job. One night after nine o'clock on a business trip to Osaka during the winter a couple of years later, I got on the Hanshin train to Ama. The reflection from the train's lights rippled in the water as we crossed the Yodo River. I went to Higashi-Naniwachō to visit the Igaya, but there was a parking lot now where the shop had been and the outside wall of the house next door was exposed. I felt a stab of pain.

I walked to Deyashiki. The sundries shop on the corner of the alley beside the apartment house was closed. I walked down the alley and went in. There seemed to be tenants on the first floor, but the whole upstairs was dark. The air was cold and dead. I walked down the corridor in the darkness. At the apartment next door where the women used to come, and the one across the hall where Horimayu-san had worked, the doors were shut. There was a hasp with a padlock on the door of the apartment where I had processed meat. I heard not a sound as I stood there in the dark.

About the Author

Choukitsu Kurumatani graduated from the German Literature Department of Keio University. He began writing fiction on the side while working at an advertising agency. His official debut as a writer came with *Shiotsubo no saji* (*Salt Spoon*), in 1992. Kurumatani has carved out a special niche as a writer of the now-rare "I-novel," an autobiographical genre of Japanese fiction.